Jean Craighead George

Ice Whale

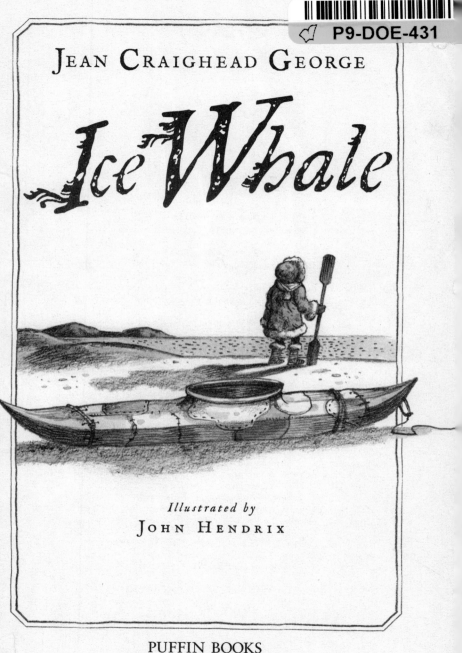

Illustrated by
John Hendrix

PUFFIN BOOKS
An Imprint of Penguin Group (USA)

For Craig

PUFFIN BOOKS
Published by the Penguin Group
Penguin Group (USA) LLC
375 Hudson Street
New York, New York 10014

USA * Canada * UK * Ireland * Australia
New Zealand * India * South Africa * China

penguin.com
A Penguin Random House Company

First published in the United States of America by Dial Books for Young Readers, 2014
Published by Puffin Books, an imprint of Penguin Young Readers Group, 2015

Copyright © 2014 by Julie Productions, Inc.

THE LIBRARY OF CONGRESS HAS CATALOGED THE DIAL BOOKS FOR YOUNG READERS EDITION AS FOLLOWS:
George, Jean Craighead, 1919–2012.
Ice whale / by Jean Craighead George.
pages cm
Summary: In 1848, ten-year-old Toozak, a Yupik Eskimo, sees a whale being born and
is told by a shaman that he and his descendants must protect that whale, which Toozak
names Siku, as long as it lives.
ISBN 978-0-8037-3745-7 (hardcover)
1. Yupik Eskimos—Juvenile fiction. [1. Yupik Eskimos—Fiction. 2. Eskimos—Fiction.
3. Bowhead whale—Fiction. 4. Whales—Fiction. 5. Human-animal relationships—Fiction.
6. Arctic regions—Fiction.] I. Title.
PZ7.G2933Ice 2014   [Fic]—dc23   2013034090

Puffin Books ISBN 978-0-14-242741-5

Printed in the United States of America

1 3 5 7 9 10 8 6 4 2

ON THE USE OF THE SYMBOLS
FOR THE WHALE SOUNDS

In the "In the Ocean" chapters, the author invented symbols that are meant to represent whale sounds. Each whale has its own individual sound, and the author worked out these different symbolic representations for that whale's name. ~~√√√√√√~~ is the symbol for Siku's name. ~~√√√√√√~~ is the symbol for the old whale, Tiguk's, name.

The sea is anything but a quiet place, and it was a riveting discovery, more than fifty years ago, that whales make sounds or calls underwater that could be recorded. Scientists capture them through underwater recording devices that pick up the sounds as vibrations in the water and convert them to signals that can be heard through speakers. The sounds can also be transcribed as written symbols, somewhat like music where tone or frequency appears as up-and-down strokes arranged on a kind of horizontal grid that indicates time. The result looks a bit like a musical score.

Undoubtedly whale sounds are meant as communication. The author invented symbols for calls that communicated danger, navigation directions, warning, and more. Toothed whales can echolocate, too, enabling them to find food, objects, and each other. We hope this explanation helps as you encounter the symbols in the book.

MAP KEY AND SCALE.

········· Toozak's Journey

– – – – Emily Toozak's Journey

SCALE 1:7,250,000

MILES
0   25   50   100   150   200

Arctic Circle

Sisualiq

Kotzebue

KOTZEBUE SOUND

Qiqiqtaq
(Shishmaref)

Wales

BERING STRAIT

DIOMEDE
ISLANDS

Nunyamo

RUSSIA

SIBERIA

Chaplino
(Unazik)

SAINT LAWRENCE
ISLAND

NORTON SOUND

BERING SEA

ANATOMY OF THE
BOWHEAD
WHALE

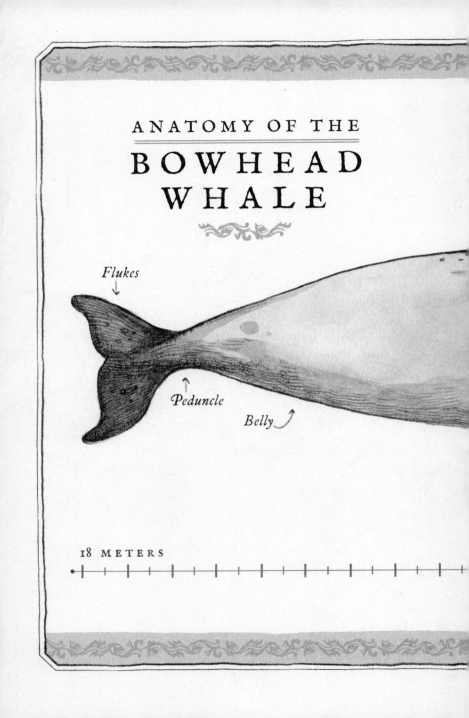

Flukes

Peduncle

Belly

18 METERS

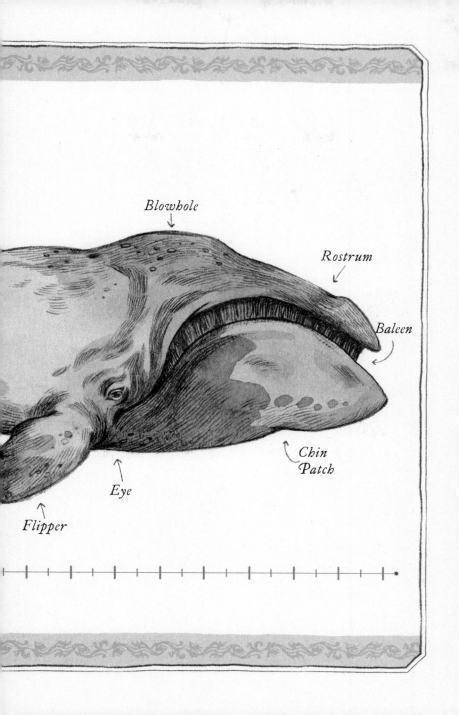

Blowhole

Rostrum

Baleen

Chin
Patch

Eye

Flipper

ICE WHALE

I

ON THE OCEAN

——— 1848 ———

The ocean waves rolled and crested, rolled and crested. Ice floes surfed them. The sun shone cold orange at 10:00 p.m.

The day, July 23. The year, 1848. The place, the Bering Strait between Alaska and Russia.

On that historic day, the whaling bark *Superior*, a chunky, blunt-nosed ship with five whaleboats hanging above her deck, set her sails into the wind. She sped due north and became the first Yankee whaler to sail through the Bering Strait. The tall black rocks of the Diomede Islands loomed in her path. Captain Thomas Roys was trying to steer clear of them.

Suddenly the wind died. The bark's sails sagged and the *Superior* came to a stop. A gull with no wind to ride alighted on the ship's midmast. Walrus barked in the distance. The terrified seamen gathered along her rail. They stared not at the rocks, but at the formidable Arctic Ocean ahead.

Only a day ago they learned that Captain Roys had paid a hundred dollars to a Russian naval officer for his charts of this ocean. Whale numbers had been decimated by two centuries of whaling in the Atlantic and Pacific. Foreign seamen who had sailed the Arctic Ocean had described it as a dangerous ocean of ice, fog, and blizzards. Frightened by the terrifying rumors of sailors freezing to death, the crew talked of mutiny.

Their captain, however, was not looking at that terrible ocean, but landward. Thirteen Eskimo *umiaqs*, large wood-frame canoes covered with walrus hide, were paddling toward the *Superior*. In them were three hundred powerful sealskin-clad Eskimo warriors ready to defend their waters and trade routes from intruders. They outnumbered his crew eight to one.

Captain Roys gritted his teeth. There was no wind to carry his ship out of the reach of the *umiaqs*, nor were there guns aboard to defend her. He took out his one, old revolver knowing it might not shoot. He wanted it at the ready anyway.

Just then a southwesterly breeze sprang up and carried the *Superior* away from the *umiaqs* and into a misty fog bank. The Eskimos grumbled—a potential trade lost. More wary of the fog than the foreigners, they turned back.

Alone and wrapped in fog, fear made the crew speak out. They complained aloud about where they were—in the dreaded Arctic Ocean! The first mate wept.

They talked of mutiny all through the short Alaskan twilight.

At dawn the fog lifted. The sun came out.

Whales were everywhere, blowing and breaching, splashing and waving their flukes. Some spy hopped or poked their heads straight up, thrusting themselves high out of the water to look at the ship. Whale footprints, whirlpools on the water made by the fluke of a whale swimming near the surface, pocked the ocean. All hands leaned against the rail, staring. They forgot their plan to mutiny.

"Lord in heaven," shouted Tom Boyd, the cabin boy. "Will you look at that!"

Captain Roys saw the whales and thanked his Maker. Leaning against the ship's wheel, he smiled. He had steered the *Superior* into a fortune.

The seamen lowered their whaleboats onto the water and rowed off to hunt the gigantic mammals that were swimming everywhere just beneath the ocean surface.

The heaviest whalers sat in the center of the twenty-eight-foot whaleboats and managed the longest oars. The other men took the seats before and behind them and rowed with shorter oars. This formation kept the eggshell-like boats gliding toward the whales.

The harpooner, Hartson, a burly man, stood in the bow. He held his harpoon high. A line was attached to it that would secure the whale to the whaleboat when it was struck. Poised, Hartson waited for a whale to come up to the surface to breathe.

No one spoke. They had long ago learned that whales could hear a whisper.

Then a whale surfaced. Hartson thrust the harpoon and struck it. It dove out of sight with the harpoon set in its back. A sea-muffled boom sounded. The seamen waited. Finally the great mammal rose slowly to the surface . . . and floated . . . dead.

"She's a right whale," cheered the harpooner. "She floats, that makes her the 'right' whale to take." He laughed and the crew pulled in the line and made it fast to the boat. The whalers now towed the whale to their ship.

When they finally brought the whale alongside the *Superior*, Captain Roys leaned over the railing and stared. The whale was fifty-five feet long with a massive head one-third the length of its body. Its blowhole sat on the highest part of its bowed head. Black in color with smooth skin, it had blunt flippers and large flukes. Captain Roys smiled. It was not a humpback whale, or even a Pacific right whale.

"We have a Greenland right whale," he shouted. "That's the blasted best!"

Greenland right whales, or bowhead whales, were the prize of commercial whalers. A bowhead had more blubber than any other whale. When this blubber was rendered into whale oil, it would burn in thousands of lamps in America. The whale's baleen, or so-called whalebone, was used to make umbrella spokes, corset stays, and hoop-skirt frames for ladies. The Atlantic right whale had helped make the United States rich and world prominent. Now, Captain Roys knew, the bowhead would do the same.

The whalers hunting the Atlantic Ocean had killed so many right whales that they were now nearly extinct. The hunters had sought new oceans and traveled into the North Pacific. There they found thousands of whales. By 1848, they had hunted the right whales in that ocean to low numbers as well.

And now there was this great discovery in the Arctic Ocean—tens of thousands of the most valuable of whales. Captain Roys's gamble had proved him right. The whalers harpooned another and another. They sang and cheered.

The blubber of these bowheads was at least a foot thick, the black skin an inch thick. The baleen— long, narrow, fringed plates composed of the same substance as fingernails that hung in the bowhead's mouth—was much longer than that of any other whale they had hunted before. The sailors looked at the bowhead in wonderment.

The slab of thick blubber was so heavy that it took eight men pulling on the hoist to lift it from the carcass. They sang chanties as they worked. Other whalers, standing on the cutting stage, a platform attached to the side of the ship, reached down with large sharp knives on long poles to cut more blubber from the whale. When it was hauled on board, it was chopped in small pieces for the tryworks, cauldrons on the ship that rendered the blubber to oil. When cooled, the whalers poured the oil in barrels.

All day long Captain Roys reaped immense profits for his sponsors, the owners, his crew, and, of course, himself. He smiled and stared at the bloody ocean and the blue-green ice floes that rode it.

The whalers worked on, hoisting strip after strip of whale blubber up to the ship's deck.

Superior's crew killed many bowhead whales that summer. By the end of August, they had filled their ship and sped south away from the freezing Arctic, through the Bering Strait to the Pacific Ocean and on to Hawaii.

When the ship arrived in Honolulu, word traveled from captain to captain, seamen to seamen, that there were thousands of bowhead whales in the western Arctic Ocean. Captains outfitted their ships that winter and prepared for the long trip back to the Arctic in the spring.

The slaughter of the great bowhead whale had begun in the western Arctic.

2

IN THE OCEAN

—— 1848 ——

Toozak, a Yup'ik Eskimo boy on Saint Lawrence Island, stared at the whaling ship just off the coast. For a long time it sat ominously on the sun-silvered ocean. Then, frightened, he paddled for shore. He must tell his father, a warrior, what he had seen. The ship had a red, white, and blue flag. Where was this ship from? What did the mariners who were on board it want?

Not far from his village he stopped. A great whale swam near him. She suddenly rolled, her flipper rising ten feet above the ocean. Through the clear water Toozak saw a baby whale slide tail first from her body. He was light gray and as long as Toozak's kayak of fourteen feet. *The baby*, he thought, *must weigh as much as all twenty dogs in my family's dog team.*

"That's a big calf," he said aloud.

Toozak bowed his head out of respect. He had seen the birth of a whale! This was a great privilege. Even his father had not seen a whale born. Only the Great Spirit could have bestowed this honor upon him.

The mother whale rolled over to her son. She nudged him gently, guiding him to the surface. The newborn took his first breath. Toozak saw a mark on his chin. It looked like an Eskimo man dancing, with one arm in the air and legs bent at the knees. Toozak stared.

That's a special whale, he thought.

Pacific herring swam around them, glistening like frost. Krill, tiny shrimp-like creatures, swirled in clouds before them. Overhead in the sky, snow geese migrated north. A seal startled by the whales dove off her ice floe and swam down out of sight. Crabs on the seafloor where the sunlight barely reached climbed over sea anemones' stinging tendrils. Fish clicked.

A whale had been born.

The mother whale sang to the bowhead community. She said, "My son has been born."

Bowhead whales are usually born in May, as the Yup'ik say, the Moon of Egg Laying. This baby whale was special. He had been born in July, the Moon of the Flowering Time of Plants. He had a destiny.

The boy, Toozak, put his ear to his paddle, and heard a high sound. It sounded like ∿∿∿∿∿, in the sea. His mother had trilled her baby's name to the water world.

∿∿∿∿∿ could swim at birth. After his first breath, he pumped his flukes, gliding to his mother's belly. Instinctively he found the protruding nipple. His mother's strong muscles pumped rich milk into his mouth. He nursed. While he fed, he and his mother loitered near Toozak. Toozak watched, fascinated. He knew this was something few people had ever witnessed.

∿∿∿∿∿ surfaced to breathe again, saw the boy, and rolled on his side to bring his eye to the surface. He looked at Toozak and Toozak looked at him, and saw his human-like eyes, with pupils, irises, and eyelids much like his own.

"You are my brother," he exclaimed. "I will call you Siku."

‿〜〜‿〜〜 stared long into Toozak's kind eyes. And something happened between them.

‿〜〜‿〜〜 returned to his mother and Toozak marveled at what he had seen. More wonderful than that, he had felt a bond with the whale he saw being born.

He was sure ‿〜〜‿〜〜 had felt that connection too. His eyes had said so. Toozak paddled to shore.

The mother did not let her youngster idle. It was learning time. She had to teach him the best coastal currents to travel on for their migration from the Bering Sea to the Beaufort Sea and back again. The round trip was 2,500 miles to their lush feeding grounds and back, with many deceptive currents. ‿〜〜‿〜〜 must learn quickly.

He learned that the sun was very important. The bright rays that shone into open water were angled. The angle and brightness were his mother's clock and calendar. They became his too. Learning to find his way was important. Just one navigational error and he might drown under the thick ice. He learned so that one day he could migrate from sea to sea without his mother. As an adult, he would one day be able to break ice three feet thick.

By the end of his first few days, ∿∿∿∿ had not only learned part of the sea route but had gained a hundred and fifty pounds and grown four inches. For the next nine months he would nurse and gain weight rapidly, nourished on just his mother's rich milk. When he stopped nursing and had to feed himself, it would be years before he grew again.

Such was the early life of a bowhead whale.

The mother and son swam on undisturbed. They saw birds when they breathed, and fish, seals, and krill when they swam. In this kaleidoscope of life they cruised slowly northward toward the top of the world, two beautiful and friendly animals.

Suddenly the mother screeched a new note,

" ∿∿∿_ _ _ _∿∿∿////∿∿∿_ "

Enemy!

A pod of orca whales came charging toward them, eager to kill and eat a sweet baby whale. ∿∿∿∿ had to learn to recognize the enemies. They had black-and-white bodies and ice-white teeth. Like him, the orcas surfaced to breathe. Like him, they were whales, but these were whales with teeth, not baleen, those filters that strained tiny food from the seawater. These whales grabbed and tore their prey. Even in whale language, they were called "killer whales."

As the orcas drew nearer ∿∿∿∿∿'s whale aunt, who had traveled nearby her pregnant and nursing sister to give her aid if she needed it, swam up to ∿∿∿∿∿. She sheltered him while his mother drove off the orcas with powerful slaps from her immense flukes—blows that could kill even an orca.

After a long while his mother came back to her sister and son. She nuzzled close to her baby.

3

ON THE LAND

SAINT LAWRENCE ISLAND
—— 1858 ——

Years passed and the boy Toozak grew to be a man of twenty. He belonged to the Yup'ik people, a skilled and ancient group of natives who lived on the islands, rivers, and coastal areas of the east coast of Siberia and the west coast of what would one day be called Alaska. Over the years young Toozak had killed many walrus, seals, and even, when he was sixteen, a polar bear on the Saint Lawrence Island, his home. He was not just a good hunter, but a superior one. Hunters were essential to life.

For the last ten summers, Toozak had seen over one

hundred Yankee whaling ships flying the red, white, and blue flag sail by his village. He saw them kill many whales that his father called "noble spirits." Other ships were foreign traders of ironware, beads, tobacco, alcohol, and woven goods. They traded these items for the Eskimos' magnificent furs and the ivory tusks of walrus. The traders rarely killed a whale, though.

One day during the Moon of the Flowering Time of Plants, around midsummer, Toozak was in his kayak off the shores of his village when he spotted a Yankee whaling ship on the ocean. Not only were its sails down despite the wind, but it was idle. That seemed unusual. He watched it.

A small white-and-blue whaleboat was lowered over its side onto the water. It rowed toward him and pulled up alongside his kayak. A Yankee leaned over the side of the boat and dangled a string of handsome blue beads before Toozak. Toozak had never been so close to a paleface seaman before.

"These are for you," a translator said in Yup'ik. "The Yankee wants you to have them."

"Aahzah," Toozak exclaimed, he hesitated. They were very nice beads and very valuable. Toozak could trade them for anything from cooking pots to knives—even guns. He took them.

The interpreter looked at Toozak with distaste. "You are only a seal hunter," he said.

"I am a good hunter," proclaimed Toozak. "I bring food to my village"

"Then you have no whales to hunt? They do not think you are worthy?" The interpreter mocked their ancient customs.

"We hunt whales," Toozak boasted, taking the bait. "We have many whales in the sound!" He gestured unconsciously with his arm, indicating a beautiful cove to the east. "But we only take what we need." He glared at the man.

The interpreter nodded, then tossed him a bag of tobacco. The Yankee whalers rowed back toward their ship.

Pleased with the beads and tobacco, Toozak paddled back toward his village. After beaching his kayak, he skinned and cut up the seal he had caught, and looked back at the ship. The white-and-blue whaleboat had not gone back to its mother ship but was rowing toward the whales in the sound.

And suddenly he knew what he had done.

"The whales!" he cried aloud. "What have I done?"

Toozak watched the whaleboat disappear around a point. A muffled explosion followed, then another and another. He trembled. Toozak had committed the worst of all crimes . . . he had led foreign men to the Eskimos' beloved whales, where they would kill them for money. He hung his head in shame.

He turned his kayak and headed toward home to ask his father what he should do. When he reached the beach hours later, he met Shaman Kumaginya, the village spirit man. He would certainly know.

"Shaman," he cried, "I have done a terrible thing. I told the Yankees where whales are. I am certain they have killed them."

The shaman frowned.

"The Whale Spirits will bring bad fortune to you," he said. "You have upset them."

Toozak bit his lip.

"I saw a whale being born when I was a boy," he said. "That puts me in high standing with the spirits, doesn't it?"

"It helps," Shaman Kumaginya said, eyeing Toozak's beautiful seal. "But perhaps it made you too proud. You were foolish.

"Come home with me and I will make a song to the spirits. They will help us know what you should do."

Toozak was very grateful. Shaman Kumaginya relieved him of his seal at his door and placed it on his meat rack away from the dogs. Toozak wanted to say that his father was waiting for Toozak to bring it to him, but he was afraid to speak. He entered the summer house. When his eyes adjusted to the low light, he saw that the walls were walrus skins. Black-and-white weasel tails decorated them. Overhead was a dome of sealskins, held up like an umbrella by willow limbs. A soot-rimmed smoke hole was in the center of the dome.

Toozak felt spirits everywhere. Shaman Kumaginya lit the stone seal-oil lamp on a sculpted plate from China. He set it on a tripod that stood under the smoke hole. On the stone he placed tinder moss and lit it. He chanted eerily and went into a deep trance.

Toozak trembled, for he knew the spirits were coming into this abode and that they could be vengeful. He had done a great wrong. If the spirits had sent a polar bear to maul his uncle for a very small misdemeanor, what would they do to him?

"The spirits are angry," the shaman finally said when he opened his eyes. "The spirits are very angry." Fear filled the room. The shaman's face was stern.

"They say you are cursed," the shaman said in an eerie voice.

"But I saw a whale being born," Toozak rasped in fear. "That makes me special."

Shaman Kumaginya threw reindeer moss on the fire and silvery oxytrope, a flower that grows only where there were no ice sheets during the Ice Age. It was magic. It could survive glaciers.

The burning mosses glowed and smoke filled the room. Then, lifting his arms to the ceiling, the shaman closed his eyes for many minutes. This gave Toozak time to look nervously for an escape from a situation that now seemed dangerous. The shaman had set several stone dishes on the floor with moss wicks burning in seal oil. He could knock them over and escape when the shaman righted them. But they might start a fire. He thought better of that idea. Some skins had been stacked at the foot of the walls—seats for guests and ghosts. They blocked his escape route under the taut walrus-skin walls. A pile of white polar-bear skins on the left of the doorway was the shaman's bed. He couldn't get out that way. There were no openings to slide through anywhere. Toozak felt the spirits inhabiting every wall and emanating from every fur.

He looked back at Shaman Kumaginya. He was still chanting with his eyes closed. His long hair fell down to his caribou calf shirt of gleaming skin. Beads and polar-bear claws hung around his neck. His face, marked with purple tattoos, seemed possessed by spirits. Toozak grew more afraid.

"To witness the birth of a whale," the shaman finally chanted, "brings the Good Spirits to you. But that is not good enough to overcome the evil of delivering the whales to the Yankees.

"You will be cursed, but because you saw a whale born, you will be spared a bit. The curse is that you must protect that whale whose birth you witnessed as long as he lives."

"How long does a whale live?" Toozak asked in a low voice.

"As long as the moon."

Toozak thought about that.

"How do I protect a whale, Shaman Kumaginya? I can't stay with him all the time."

"*Eii*, that is for you to find out." The shaman rubbed his hands together. "You have done a terrible thing."

"I know, I know." Toozak bent his head. "But I'm a seal hunter and I do not know how to protect a whale."

"Learn," the older man said.

Toozak's hands grew cold. His mind was racing.

The shaman saw his misery and added, "If a whale saves a Toozak, your family will be free of the curse."

"How can a whale save anybody?" Toozak asked in confusion.

"It is said that an ancient great whale hunter lives to the north. You must learn from him," the shaman replied. "Now leave our village. Take the curse with you."

"Where will I go?"

"To the north. Follow your whale. Protect him."

"Then I will find the ancient whale hunter. But, how will he help me protect Siku?" Toozak said.

The shaman looked closely at Toozak. "Eskimos love the whale best. Whales give them food, shelter, utensils, life. Whale hunters know more about the whales than anyone. And, the whales know them, too. That is how a whale knows when to give himself. Go. Learn."

Shaman Kumaginya had one more thing to say.

"The whale may live longer than you. It is said that they live two human lifetimes." The rising smoke obscured him for a moment. "Give the name Toozak to your firstborn. Tell him to protect and respect the whale. His life might not be long enough either, so he must name *his* son Toozak. And the next generation and the next must be named Toozak, until the whale dies or saves a Toozak."

Shaman Kumaginya threw some more reindeer moss on the fire. In the smoke that now arose around them, he took down his dance drum. He beat two deep notes.

"*Aye, ya, ya, aye, aye.* You betrayed the whales," he chanted, then stepped into the thick smoke and became, to Toozak's eyes, only a voice and a drumbeat.

Toozak was terrified.

Shaman Kumaginya paused and said, "The spirits say if you can lift the stones in the Circle of Stones in the village, the curse will disappear."

"I am strong," Toozak whispered.

"Go now," Toozak heard the shaman's wavering voice say.

Toozak put his hands over his ears and ran toward the door. *I have seen you born, Siku,* he said to himself. *I have looked into your human-like eyes. We are brothers. You are my whale. I will protect you as long as I live even if I can't break the curse!* Toozak shuddered, the shaman's words still ringing in his ears. "Now leave our village. Take the curse with you."

Toozak ran right to the center of the village. There, thirty stones were arranged in a circle. They had been placed in this spot for the hunters to pick up every day to make them strong.

I must pick up all of them, even the heavy one in the middle. Toozak gritted his teeth.

Smoke was rising from the holes that had been cut into the homes of skin and driftwood much like the shaman's. The townsfolk were preparing food. Toozak was not thinking of eating. He stepped into the ring of stones and lifted one, then the next. At number twenty he fell to his knees. He tried again, straining every muscle and tendon.

"I can't," he said, and walked slowly home, his muscles trembling with exhaustion. Once he was home, he told his father and mother what he had done.

"I showed Yankee whalers where some whales were feeding," he said. "They killed them. This was a terrible thing to do, and because of it, the shaman says I must leave the village and learn from an ancient hunter how to protect Siku."

His parents held their son.

A family was leaving the island on the difficult crossing to the Siberian mainland in their skin boat. They had room for Toozak, his dogs and gear, all the things that he needed for his journey. His parents were distressed at his leaving, but they agreed that the shaman must be right and so they helped Toozak get ready. They put dog packs on the two dogs, named Woof and Lik. Toozak filled and strapped onto one pack a bow, some arrows, a seal hook, fire tools, a knife, a net, and a sleeping fur. He also brought his harpoon, his ice chisel, and his lance. With these tools he could survive anywhere in the Arctic.

Then Toozak went to his father's ice cellar, which had been dug into the frozen soil. He climbed down the ladder to the bottom of the big, icy room and brought up some frozen fish for himself, his dogs, and other travelers. He was sorry he would not be able to go fishing and replace what he had taken from his parents. His mother helped him fill the other pack with fish and dried food.

He was ready to leave. As he was tying a towline to his kayak from the back of the boat, his sister ran out of their home. She handed him an exquisite sable that their father had gotten in a trade with Siberian Eskimos for a polar-bear skin. He had given the sable to her. Now she presented it to Toozak and hugged him closely.

"Its spirit will go with you," she whispered. "It will make you smart and skilled like the sable."

Toozak hugged her long and hard. His parents stepped forward to embrace their son. They knew they might never see him again. They all broke down in tears and sobbed. Wiping the tears from his face, Toozak stepped into the skin boat. His journey had begun.

Once I am on the Siberian mainland, I will paddle north

to Naukan, staying near shore, he thought. *The dogs will
tow me when it is possible; otherwise they will run along
the shore and follow me. Sometimes they will ride with me
in the kayak. There I will cross to the Diomedes and on to
the Inupiat nations to the east in Alaska. I'll find a village
and wait for the sea to freeze. I will make a sled of willows
and driftwood to use on the ice and snow.*

Eventually I will go on to Tikiġaq [TEE-key-gak] (the
village that would one day be called Point Hope). *If I can
get there before the sea ice melts and the Yankee whalers
arrive, I will warn Siku. I will protect him as the shaman has
willed.*

But how did someone warn a whale away? He would
have to ask the elders and hunters.

Suddenly he smiled. Years ago, when he was at one of
the annual trade fairs at Sisualiq [SIS-ou-ah-lik] "place that
has begula whales," he had met a lovely girl named Qutuuq
[KOO-took]. She lived in Tikiġaq. It was impossibly far from
his village, but it was near to where he was going now. He
had thought he might never see her again.

For a moment he imagined he would find her, and maybe
he would marry her, and the two of them could protect Siku
together.

He turned his thoughts to Tikiġaq.

"Thank you, Siku, because of you I have hope."

And for the first time since he had revealed to the Yan-kees where the whales were hiding, his spirit lifted.

4

ON THE LAND

—— 1858 ——

Sailing through the ice floes and rough seas in the big skin boat, Toozak and the family made their way slowly to Unazik, on the Russian mainland. They lived on seal and walrus that they harpooned among the ice floes during their three-day journey. They were lucky there were no storms to slow their progress. The remarkable skin boat rode the ocean swells perfectly, like the graceful walrus it was made of. Thousands of seabirds flew overhead, ice floes freckled the immense sea. Toozak sat in the bow immersed in the beauty, power, and excitement of the journey.

When they arrived at the mainland, Toozak paid the family with half the dried fish he had brought with him. He found his relatives in Unazik, and they celebrated his visit for several days. The Saint Lawrence Yup'ik were closely connected to the Siberian Yup'ik families along the Russian coast. They traded back and forth and often married.

Finally it was time to head north up the coast with his two dogs, his kayak, and all his gear. He moved north, sometimes paddling, sometimes being towed by Lik and Woof along the beach, and sometimes, when the seas were rough, dragging his kayak and gear.

His progress was slow but the scenery was new and exciting with coastal mountains, grizzly bears, and grasses that were turning gold. He met many Siberian Yup'ik and Chukchi families along the coast. He saw their dramatic-looking monuments, made of giant whalebones standing against the sky—a testament to their enduring cultures. Often, he would be invited to hunt with them, contributing his skill in exchange for a warm, dry place to sleep. He also learned a great deal about whales and whaling from hunters with great knowledge.

At Nunyamo, he made preparations for the dangerous crossing to the Diomede Islands and on to the North American continent. The Diomedes were the hub of trade between Asia and North America. The negotiations could be tense, as Toozak was bargaining with the wealthiest and most powerful Eskimos. They did not tolerate those who might interfere with their commerce.

Toozak approached a village elder.

"May I travel with you in your *umiaq* to the Diomedes?" he asked respectfully. Most traders spoke many languages, and he hoped he would be understood.

"What can you offer in return?" the elder replied in Yup'ik.

"I have very little," Toozak replied, "but I am a good hunter and hard worker."

The elder, dressed in immaculate skins, grumbled and then nodded toward the huge *umiaq* that was being loaded. Toozak sighed with relief. A ride in the traders' large *umiaq* with many others would be much safer than trying to make the dangerous crossing himself in his small kayak with two dogs.

They traveled through the swift currents to the remarkable Big Diomede Island. Here was a whole village and society perched on near-vertical cliffs. Seabirds swirled, seals were numerous. It was a magical place.

They unloaded their trade goods and Toozak worked hard carrying the amazing variety of goods up the steep hills to the dwellings.

The next day, they reloaded the skin boat with more trade goods and continued across the treacherous currents of the Bering Strait. Toozak was tired and inwardly fretting about the trip that lay ahead.

Sea life was everywhere. The skin boat rose and surfed the huge waves. A ringed seal surfaced near the boat, stared, and dove in an instant. Then he heard the unmistakable whoosh of a bowhead's blow. He suddenly stood up and touched his cheek. Just as he did so, one of the whales rolled—and to his astonishment there it was . . . the mark of the Eskimo dancer on its chin.

"Siku, I will help you," Toozak whispered.

The whale dove and was gone, headed south.

They continued on to the village of Wales on the Alaskan coast. Villagers came out and pulled the boat ashore. It had been an incredible trip, and Toozak thanked the traders profusely for their help. He was in a new land, with new people and the prospect of a new life.

He traveled northeast up the coast of the peninsula toward the village of Qigiqtag [Ke-GIK-tuk, later known as Shishmaref], where he met with the townsfolk and exchanged stories of his travels.

Toozak put his kayak in the water at the village beach. After harnessing the boisterous dogs and attaching them to a long line, he threw his packs in the kayak and got in. Singing happily, he navigated with the rudder, with the dogs, tails high, towing him along a chain of barrier islands north of the village. Every mile, every beach, put distance between Toozak and that terrifying shaman and brought him closer to his lovely friend. He knew that he would protect Siku, somehow.

> *"Siku, Siku,*
> *I will protect you.*
> *I will protect you.*
> *My loving whale,*
> *I will protect you."*

His feelings for Siku were warm. Now Siku was Toozak's whale. Toozak had seen him being born. He would protect him. He didn't know exactly how, but he would. He would find the ancient whale hunter. This whale hunter would help him protect Siku. And maybe then Toozak would know what to do. His heart pounded. He and Siku were brothers.

Now and then Toozak came ashore to eat and sleep. Late one afternoon, around dusk, he noticed a flock of auklets flying toward the deep water of the ocean where they spend the winter. This was a good sign. The freeze was coming, which would make traveling easier.

Three sleeps later he pulled ashore on the southern cape of Kotzebue Sound. The dogs leaped out of the kayak, nearly upsetting it. Steadying himself, Toozak stepped out onto a stony shore. He looked north over the gleaming water of the sound.

"Look, Woof," he said, stroking the dog's head. "Kotzebue Sound is still open. We will stay here till it freezes."

He looked around, knowing he had lots of time before him. The landscape was different from that of his home. The shrubs were smaller and twisted by the wind and snow. In the distance, snow-tipped mountains shone white and turquoise. Clouds of birds flew south.

What was best, he saw, was that he was not far from the shore-hugging currents heading toward the Kotzebue Sound. Siku would travel north on them in the spring. He, Toozak, would scare off Siku's enemies, the Yankees and the orcas. The thought gave him great hope.

"Siku," he called out. "I will protect you."

He threw out his chest and looked seaward. Then, putting down his sleeping furs and using his beloved sable as a pillow, he took out some raw fish for his supper.

An Eskimo man in fur garments approached him. Toozak was nervous. Had he crossed a clan territory line? In some areas, it was the custom to kill unknown travelers. Was the man coming to kill him?

"What are you doing here, young man?" The Eskimo

asked him this question in four different languages before Toozak responded.

Using his hands and the few Inupiat words he had learned from the traders, he said, "I am waiting for the sound to freeze so that I can cross."

"It will be weeks till that occurs," the man said clearly in Yup'ik when he realized Toozak was from that nation. He had a kind face and he smiled when he said, "Come stay with me and my family. Can you hunt? The hunting time is here and I could use some help."

Toozak nodded and accepted the offer. He carried his kayak out of the wind, then called Woof and Lik to his side and joined the man.

The man's home was a large sealskin abode whose walls were decorated with tools and a grizzly bear skin. Toozak immediately felt at home.

Within a week's time, he had shot a caribou with his bow and arrow and caught many fish for the man. The man's wife was so grateful she not only gave him a portion of the caribou but helped him build a sled from willow limbs and driftwood. The sled was big enough to hold all of Toozak's possessions, including his kayak. He was pleased.

"My husband is getting old and is not as good a hunter

as you," she said when they had finished making the sled. "I am glad for your skill."

"And I am glad for yours," Toozak said, looking at the graceful sled she had helped to create.

Two weeks later, the sound waters began forming pancake ice, the round disks that precede the freeze-up. Cold winds blew down from the North Pole. The ice thickened. One day during the Moon of Freezing, October, when summer was over, Toozak chopped a hole in the sound ice with the stone ax the wife had given him. The ice was one foot thick—plenty thick to travel on. That day he told the family it was time for him to leave.

Early the next morning, despite stinging winds, Toozak lashed his possessions on the new sled, put his kayak on top of it, and hitched up the dogs. The sable he put under his parka, where he could hug it to ease his aching muscles. There were good spirits in it he was sure, just as his sister had said.

"Kiita, Kiita," he called to Woof and Lik. "Ah—eeee," he called to his friends, and waved.

By late evening on the second day, he had mushed across the sound and arrived at the village of Sisualiq. The villagers came out of their homes, and Toozak was relieved to see that they greeted him joyously. Women in caribou parkas fed him, the men asked him for news, and finally all wished to know where he was going. When he said to Tikiġaq, one elder was delighted. A well-traveled man, he began telling Toozak the best way to go.

"Take the old trade route," he said. "It goes over land. When you get to the Igichuk Hills, leave that route and take to the sea ice. It will be thick enough to travel on by then—and a lot smoother.

"It's a beautiful run to Tikiġaq from the Hills at this time of year," he went on. "Little shrubs peeking through the snow. Caribou are scattered through the hills, they make the dogs happy. Very glorious.

"But stay tonight," added the elder. "Sleep this darkness in my home."

The wind was now blowing snow and ice crystals. Toozak accepted the elder's hospitality. He followed his new friend to a large underground winter home. It was dug into the earth and domed with sod. One entered it by taking a tunnel down, then climbing up into the home. After tying Woof and Lik to a gnarled bush and feeding them frozen fish, Toozak followed his host through the *qanitchat* [KA-nit-chuk], an airlock tunnel that captured the cold air to keep it from penetrating into the home.

As he came out of the tunnel into the house, he was welcomed by three young children and their mother. They greeted him warmly and showed him where to put his sleeping fur on the floor. Quietly he placed his sable on top of it. The sable had become his "good spirit." He felt it would help him protect Siku, since the sable was an intelligent animal with a noble spirit.

When Toozak was settled, the mother, smiling broadly, handed him an iron frying pan that was filled with bubbling walrus soup. The soup was thick with fat and the meat was as tender as young caribou. While he ate, the husband asked him many questions—questions about fishing, questions about winterberries and whether he had seen any caribou. Had the snowy owls left?

Just before dark some important-looking men entered the home to talk to Toozak. They were dressed in elaborately decorated parkas of various furs. Around their necks hung bear claws and weasel tails, symbols of their importance.

"Have you seen the American sailing ships?" they asked.

Toozak nodded.

"Do they harbor evil spirits?" an elder asked.

Toozak said he didn't know. Talking about evil spirits made him uneasy.

"Do they come to trade?" asked one man. "Will they trade our furs for liquor and tobacco?" He smiled.

"They do have goods to trade," Toozak said, "like beads and tobacco. But, be careful, they come mostly to kill our whales. They also take the ivory tusks from our walrus. They kill many—many more than they need, I think. I have seen the ocean red with blood."

"That's why there are fewer whales and walrus," observed an elder, shaking his head. "Our people will starve because of these men."

The men departed at midnight, and at the following sunrise Toozak was ready to leave. The mother gave him a cooked snowshoe hare and the children gave him fish for the dogs. He rode away waving.

"*Kiita*, Woof. *Kiita*, Lik," he shouted. The snow made the runners of the sled squeal as they slid across it. Icy gusts buffeted Toozak and sent snow spiraling over the willows and land. It was thirty below zero, and rime ice crusted his eyebrows and ruff. But he was warm in his parka and had a full belly. Smiling, he rode into the snow clouds.

The Yankees have gone south for the winter. Siku is in the Bering Sea, far away from the greedy whalers, Toozak said to himself. *I feel him. He is swimming leisurely. He is rolling gently. He is in his winter home.*

Many days later, Toozak reached Tikiġaq. The sun barely rose before it set, for it was the Moon of Sitting, the beginning of winter.

Toozak was wide-eyed. This was the biggest town he had ever seen, a famous whaling and market town. It had become a trading center, with the Americans, Irish, Cape Verdeans, Germans, Russians, Portuguese, and Japanese. They traded blue beads, tobacco, hardware, and liquor for the Eskimos' furs and ivory. But Toozak was not looking for trade. He drove to the edge of town, let Woof and Lik off their harnesses, and tied them to a stake he had hammered into the ground. After throwing each a fish in celebration of the journey's end, he walked up to an Inupiat man who was sitting nearby. He wore handsome Russian boots and a stunning polar-bear parka.

"Do you know where the Qingak family lives?" he asked.

"Suuurreeesh," the man answered, and Toozak saw why his speech was slurred. An empty liquor container lay at his side. The white men were trading liquor for furs. Drunken men cannot hunt and their families sometimes starve.

Toozak walked away slowly toward the village. Presently he came to a boy who was playing with an Eskimo yo-yo—that remarkable invention that allows two sealskin balls to swing in opposite directions at the same time.

"Where does the Qingak family live?" he asked. "Can you tell me?"

"Follow me," said the boy, spinning the yo-yo around his head. Toozak went back for his sled and dogs and walked with the yo-yo spinner to a large sod-covered home. There were piles of caribou and whale bones stacked in the yard.

"Siku," he whispered. "Perhaps I will find the ancient whale hunter in this town."

"This is where the Qingak family lives," the boy said, and went on down the path not missing a spin of his yo-yo.

Toozak was looking at the whale bones and caribou antlers that had been placed in front of the home.

So many bones, he thought. *That means that Qutuuq's father is an important man—a good hunter.*

While he was thinking about how to introduce himself, Qutuuq's father, Kakinnaaq [KA-kin-ak], pushed back the bearskin door and hailed him.

"Young man," he said, "my daughter says she met you at the trading market. That you are far from your home and a very good hunter."

"Yes, I am far from home," said Toozak. "I seek a whale with the mark of a dancer on his chin. Do the ice whales come close to shore here?"

"They do—and I have seen that very one." Kakinnaaq

smiled. "He is special—a very beautiful whale. Will he give himself to you?"

"No, no. He is too young. He must grow. I seek him so I can protect him. Until he dies," he added under his breath. And he explained the shaman's curse.

"Until your whale returns in spring, come hunt with me," Kakinnaaq said. "The long night is near. I could use your help."

Toozak took his bow and arrows from his sled. He covered his lance and gleaming sable fur with his bags and followed Kakinnaaq as he walked toward the tundra. After he had shot five ptarmigan cocks to Kakinnaaq's two, Kakinnaaq invited him to his home.

5

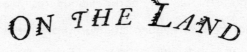

ON THE LAND

—— 1858–1859 ——

In the middle of Moon of Forming Frost under the Roof—the middle of winter—it was night for twenty-four hours a day. This was when the North Star, called the "never move" star by the northern peoples, was visible while the sky was dark.

At "never move" time, Toozak laughing and teasing, chased Qutuuq across the floor of the large home. They ended up near her bed. Then Kakinnaaq jumped from his sleeping furs and chased Toozak away.

For many nights Toozak chased Qutuuq, laughing, to her bed only to be shouted away by Kakinnaaq. Then came the day, when the sun had arisen only briefly before it set, that

Toozak thrust his lance into a lone musk oxen's heart. The Kakinnaaq family not only had delicious fresh meat but a musk-oxen hide, the warmest of all furs. On that night of darkness, Kakinnaaq let Toozak reach Qutuuq's bed and this time climb in. With that, Toozak and Qutuuq were married in the ancient tradition.

The next day Toozak sang to himself,

"Oh, Siku, my ice whale,

I am so happy.

So happy.

You have brought me good fortune.

Aye, aye, aye

I will protect you as long as I live.

I will live right here where you pass by.

Aye, aye, aye."

Spring came and the whales began migrating north. Toozak every day climbed a big ice pressure ridge. He wanted to see Siku and noted all the whales that went by.

But Toozak did not see the whale and he was discouraged. Then he thought that maybe Siku was staying away from the whalers and protecting himself. He smiled.

One day, when the sun was shining longer, Toozak went walrus hunting. He killed and brought home a large one.

"They are scarce," he said to his father-in-law. "Only two walrus instead of two thousand were on that ice floe."

Kakinnaaq frowned. "I have seen that too," he said. "Only a few walrus ride the ice floes past our village. Some evil has fallen upon us. I will ask our shaman what it might be."

"Not the shaman." Toozak clutched his sable in fear. "He is all-powerful and will know what I did—betrayed those whales in the sound." He bent his head. Kakinnaaq walked out the door.

In a few minutes he was back from the shaman's home.

"The shaman is drunk," he said.

Toozak was shocked. Then he began to think, if the shaman had magic powers, why couldn't he use them to stop himself from drinking? He decided if a shaman could get drunk, then maybe shamans didn't have magic powers after all. But he was not sure. One way or the other, though, he knew that he would protect Siku. He was his beloved whale, bonded to him—his brother. He would wait for Siku. He would watch.

Kakinnaaq thought more about Siku. "I am old and cannot help you protect Siku. Just stay connected to his spirit and he will tell you when he faces danger. We need the animals that give us life—and they need us."

✿ ✿ ✿

Working nonstop for days, Toozak's new wife, Qutuuq, and the other village women cut, sewed, and stretched the seal-skin over the *umiaq* frame. It was tedious, difficult work. The women were covered in seal oil, and the smell of the fermented skins was overpowering.

While the women worked, Toozak took one of the walrus skins a short distance from his in-laws' house and propped it up with driftwood poles. Then he gathered some caribou skins that he had dried and scraped. Together with the walrus skin, they were hung to form a big square. He tied them to the driftwood crossbeams with sinew. A home was taking shape. Finally he made a roof of canvas from the sail of a wrecked Yankee whaleboat and propped it up with baleen strips . . . and the newlyweds had their first home. A year passed and spring came again. The whales would return.

Into this home on a spring day, Toozak II was born. His father sang.

"Sleep, little Toozak.

Sleep, sleep, sleep.

Siku is coming

Through the blue waves."

The next day, a neighbor showed Toozak his newfangled shoulder gun, aimed it toward the ocean, and pulled the trigger. The loud BOOM surprised them both. Toozak was alarmed. Eskimos now had Yankee whaling guns. At home he had seen that this explosive whale gun could do whales great harm. Siku would be coming north. He might even be near. But it was important for Tikiġaq to harvest whales so Toozak understood that Siku might offer himself to a worthy hunter.

Toozak walked out onto the sea ice. Sitting down on an enormous block of pale blue ice, he watched the open lead, a black streak of open water in the white ice. Whales swam by. After a long wait, the water swirled and a whale breached. On his chin was a white spot in the shape of a dancing Eskimo. Siku was in the Tikiġaq hunting area.

"Siku," Toozak shouted loud enough to warn him. "Go. Go.!" The whale seemed to understand, and dove. Large ripples marked Siku's hasty retreat.

Toozak knew that frightening whales away would draw the wrath of the whalers, but none were around to hear him. He prayed that another whale would give himself to the hunters of Tikiġaq and Siku would be spared.

"_ _ ～～～～ _ _ _ ～～～ _ _" came from the water like a wind song.

"Siku, what are you saying?" Toozak wondered aloud as he lightly touched his cheek.

He waited many hours . . . no more whales came by.

Siku was safe.

Toozak smiled. He did not want to leave this magnificent ice world. He had found Siku. And he had found a home.

The ocean was blinding white but for the blue-black ice leads. Puffy clouds ringed the horizon. Geese flew north. Ivory gulls darted over the ice floes and Arctic terns called their rasping *keeeyurr.* The Great Spirit was kissing the world.

"My home and yours, Siku." Toozak whispered so as not to frighten other whales.

Days later, the whale hunters of Tikiġaq caught two whales for the community. Siku was far to the north.

6

ON THE OCEAN

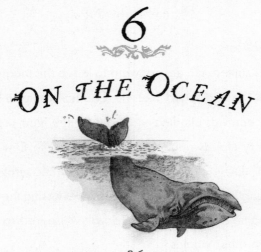

—— 1861 ——

Tom Boyd, once a lowly cabin boy, had spent years and years working his way up through the ranks and was now the captain of the whaling ship *Trident*. He ordered all her sails unfurled to the wind.

He lifted his head into the Arctic wind and breathed deeply. Tom had attended public school in New Bedford, Massachusetts, and at twenty-two married lovely Anne Dana. That year he signed on to a fishing vessel and worked his way up the ranks as he learned to sail in storm and calm—preparation for a trip to the Arctic.

Now at last his dream was fulfilled. He was a captain and in the Arctic.

By his side was the boy Tom II, his son, as wide-eyed and excited as the captain had once been.

With the winds behind her, the ship sped north through the Bering Strait on to the Arctic Ocean. White ice floes freckled the dark blue water. Gulls flew in arcs and seals slept on the land-fast ice that was frozen to the bottom near the shores.

Days later, they came upon a small group of bowhead whales in the open ocean. A crew went in pursuit, and harpooned and killed one. After muscle-straining work, the men hauled it to the *Trident* and began preparing it for butchering.

Big Henry, a harpooner, and seven other whalers cut off a thick sheet of blubber. Then, all together, they hoisted it to the deck.

"Small," grumbled Big Henry of the whale. "We've taken most of the big ones." He leaned on his ten-foot-long pole with the whale-flensing knife on the end. "Wasn't like this in forty-eight when I first came to the Arctic Ocean."

John, the first mate, joined the captain, Tom II, and Big Henry to watch the action.

"I fear," John said thoughtfully, "that the whalers have harvested too many bowheads."

Tom II pushed back his parka hood and turned to John. "Have whalers taken that many?"

"Yes. Look at all the whaling ships out there." He gestured seaward. "I've been here when whales were to the right, left, above, and underneath. Now it's hard to find even one—and this is only thirteen years after the first whale was taken."

"This is the first time I've been in the Arctic Ocean," Tom II said. "Mother insisted she go along with Father when he said he would be gone three years." Tom II smiled. "And I had to come along too. I'm glad we did. This ocean's really different." He gestured to the blue-and-white world, to the birds flying overhead and seals sliding off ice floes and the pack ice that had formed a frozen quilt on top of the water.

Suddenly Tom II's eyes rested on the eye of the dead whale. It was open, and looking at him. He was gripped by a piercing sadness.

"Great whale," he murmured, but not loud enough for anyone to hear, "I am sorry."

As the whalers started cutting the blubber, he averted his eyes. He did not want to see the butchering.

The ship suddenly rolled. Tom II lost his footing and stumbled close to the tryworks, those brick structures which held the huge iron pots that were kept ready for rendering the blubber to oil.

The ship straightened. Tom II recovered his balance.

"Big Henry," he said, pointing to the tryworks, "do we really need to boil down the blubber? It's hard dangerous work."

"Aye," Big Henry answered, "we can carry far more whale oil when we render it here at sea. Makes more room for walrus tusks." He glanced out at the pack ice. It was moving toward them. He frowned.

There was a crunching sound. The ship rolled sharply to starboard. Tom II lost his footing again, grabbed the brace on the mainmast, and hung on. The pack ice had ridden in and now was pressed against the ship, pushing it toward the land-fast ice. Again the *Trident* righted herself and Tom II scurried down the ladder to his father's quarters. His mother looked up.

"I hope we finish here soon and get clear of the ice," Tom II said. "There is ice all around us." He sat down at his desk and picked up a book. He wanted to forget that steep roll.

His mother said, "When you're done with that, I'll hear your spelling."

Tom II looked down at his book.

In moments, he lifted his head. He could tell his mother was nervous about the rolling ship too.

"We're drifting," he said.

The ship jolted to a stop.

"Now we're not."

"Do your lessons," his mother said.

A screaming hiss sounded. Tom II jumped up, threw back the door, and ran up the steps to the deck. He met his father striding toward the helm.

"What's happening?" Tom II asked.

"We're having a little trouble," Captain Boyd explained when he saw his son's anxious face. "A storm is coming. The wind is pushing us against a big ice floe." He hurried on. Tom II followed him to the bridge.

"This is the Arctic," Boyd said. "There are always dangers here." He took the wheel.

The *Trident*'s sails filled, and it changed course, then slowly gained speed. Captain Boyd steered around the ice floes and out into the open ocean. They could still see the shore. Outwardly he appeared confident, inwardly he shook. He knew the treachery of the pack ice.

Tom II sat down on a coil of rope. He had heard many stories of ships crushed by the ice.

"We need wood for the tryworks," Captain Boyd shouted when he saw his boy sitting. "Go help Big Henry get some."

Tom II ran down to the deck. He could hear the sound of the pumps. That meant water was coming in somewhere. He climbed down into the hold where two men were still straining to operate the pumps, and found Big Henry stuffing oakum into the leaks. The flow stopped.

"Now I get wood," Big Henry said to Tom II. "The fires in the ovens are almost out."

"Wood, here? But there's only ice!"

"Many logs are washed down the big rivers and drift around the Arctic Ocean. They eventually cast up on shore, where we get them. The Eskimos build boats and homes with them." On the deck Henry lowered the dory and slid down a rope to it.

While Tom and John watched from the deck, he came ashore near a spruce log that John had spotted. It was silvery gray from years of battering against the ice. Big Henry chopped it in quarters and tossed it into the boat.

Tom II grabbed John's arm and pointed. An Eskimo was coming toward Henry. His polar-bear mukluks were crunching on the beach stones; his parka hood was pushed back from his angry face. He quickened his pace. Out of the low shrubs came four more Eskimos.

The Eskimos came on. Henry quickly threw a couple of heavy logs into the boat, pushed off, and began to row.

The five Eskimos raised their bows and arrows. Big Henry just rowed, putting distance between them, and returned to the *Trident*.

"Were you scared?" Tom II asked Big Henry.

"Yes, but you know what scares me more?" he replied. "This ocean. This weather. This ice." He hoisted the wood to John on the deck.

Snow blew out of the sky. Ice pellets pummeled the ship. Gusty winds blew and *Trident*'s sails were trimmed. A Bering Sea storm was upon them. Other than ice, Arctic storms were what the whalers dreaded most. The deck was awash in huge seas and whale oil from broken casks.

Through the storm the *Trident* limped its way out of the Bering Sea south toward Hawaii.

7

IN THE OCEAN

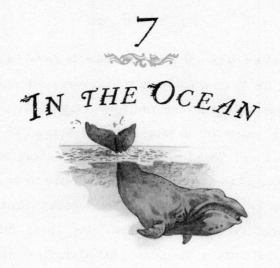

——— 1862 ———

〜〜〜〜〜 *joined a group of male bowheads on their* spring migration. His mother had gone ahead with the other adult females. Their babies, born during the migration, swam beside them. The mother whales slowed their swimming speed to the calves' pace.

〜〜〜〜〜 was now thirteen years old and had left his mother's company long ago. Siku's mother was escorting a nursing daughter and teaching her about killer whales and whaling ships. The ships were following them along coastal currents to their summer home. There were hundreds of them.

〜〜〜〜〜 swam more rapidly than he ever

had before to escape the ships. Near Barrow, he swam along the Barrow Canyon, which was scattered with brittlestars, anemones, and snow crabs.

Fish swam by in large schools. Masses of clams opened and closed their shells. The seafloor seemed to move as they crawled from one place to another.

‿‿⌒⌒⌒‿‿⌒⌒⌒ had seen few walrus during his lifetime. Whalers had killed over three hundred thousand of them. The ocean life had changed markedly in the thirteen years of Yankee whale and walrus hunting. Siku could feel the change.

Beyond Barrow, ‿‿⌒⌒⌒‿⌒⌒⌒'s group joined another small group of male bowheads and crossed into the Beaufort Sea. This group had avoided the whalers by following an old and wise whale named ⌒⌒⌒⌒⌒⌒⌒ or Tiguk. Bowhead whales do not have a single leader, as men and wolves have, just wise elders whom the younger whales follow and learn from. Tiguk was 115 years old.

After a two-week swim from Barrow through shattered ice flows, they arrived at their destination— the Eastern Beaufort Sea. It was spring, and briefly the sea's waters were as clear as air. The whales relaxed near the pack ice that glowed a deep turquoise blue in the sun. They were less than a thousand miles from the North Pole and three hundred miles from the magnetic pole. ⁓⌇⌇⁓ rolled and tumbled among the ice floes. He spun to the bottom of the sea and back up to the surface.

The bowhead whales came to the Eastern Beaufort Sea for the zooplankton, those large masses of shrimp-like krill and copepods that were their food. The seawater was as rich with this food as it had been for millions of years.

⁓⌇⌇⁓ opened his mouth wider than an *umiaq* and took in a ton of plankton mass and seawater. He closed it, letting most of the water pour out the corners. The plankton was efficiently strained from the rest of the seawater by the hairs on the 640 baleen plates hanging from the roof of his mouth. He pressed out the remaining water with his tongue. He swallowed a hundred pounds of krill. This was his first good meal in a long time.

⁓⌇⌇⁓ ate well that summer, and played under the water. Ice hung down from the melting floes like the stalactites on the roof of a cave. He breached with his friends. They splashed each other and dove together, and, as if in a choreographed whale dance, spiraled down to the depths and up again. They swam on their backs and rolled.

～～ᴟᴧᴧᴧ～ᴧᴧᴧ found a huge log and pushed it back to his gang. They shoved it from one to another, tried to sink it, and finally gave up.

～～ᴧᴧᴧᴧ～ᴧᴧᴧ loved to play and feed in the upwellings where bottom water comes to the surface. He rolled and tumbled in them, and when he was tired, he lay still at the surface listening to the music of the sea, blowing softly as he breathed in and out. He heard bowheads' chatter, clams and fish chirp, shrimp click, and snails blip. The sounds were soothing. This was home.

After three months of eating and playing, ～ᴧᴧᴧᴧ～ᴧᴧᴧ heard a shrill treble note. " - - - - - - - - - - - \\\\\\\\\\\ _ _ _ ⌐ - - \\\\\\\\\\\\\\\\\"

Prepare to go south.

ᴧᴧᴧᴧ～ᴧᴧᴧᴧ had sent the message. He had seen a change in the angle of the sun's rays slanting into the seawater. It said to him that new ice would be forming soon. The almost-three-month-long day had ended. Brief nights followed, then longer and longer nights. When the surface of the Beaufort Sea turned frothy with crystals ᴧᴧᴧᴧ～ᴧᴧᴧᴧ shrilled his "turn

south" message again, and added, "〰〰〰〰〰〰〰."
Go!

〰〰〰〰 swallowed a last mouthful of zoo-plankton and joined 〰〰〰〰. He swam slowly beside the immense eighty-five-ton whale until they reached a violet band of seawater. It was the cold current circling down from the high-latitude Arctic Sea to join the current from the Eastern Beaufort. 〰〰〰〰 and 〰〰〰〰 swam with it. In this way, they were swept west toward Russia on their autumn route.

Other whales joined them until thirty individuals, including 〰〰〰〰's mother and five other females, made up their group. Male and female bowheads mingled for the fall migration and some chose mates.

〰〰〰〰 was just beginning to be interested in females. He swam beside one all the way to Barrow, the two of them calling back and forth. Ten days later, they neared Tikiġaq. Siku noticed a young Eskimo fishing from a boat some distance from land. He left his friend to seek out the man. He knew him. He circled the man, just to be sure. He recognized his face and sensed he was a good man. 〰〰〰〰

had learned this early in life. For whales, this understanding could mean escaping a dangerous situation. Orcas and red, white, and blue Yankee whaling ships were danger. But ～〰〰〰 knew this man with the kind eyes was good.

The Eskimos have a two thousand-year relationship with the bowhead. They believe the whale has a spirit and knows the hunter and even what he is thinking. Whales only offer themselves to worthy hunters.

～〰〰〰 spy hopped to look at Toozak again. Then he dove and spanked his tail on the surface of the water.

"〰〰＿〰〰," Siku shrilled.

I remember you, boy of the kind eyes.

He breached in gladness. Toozak saw the mark on his chin that resembled an Eskimo dancer.

"Siku, go," he called, and clapped his hands. "Go deep. The Yankees are out whaling. They say that whales are always listening. Listen, Siku, hear me and go!"

～〰〰〰 waved his fluke and swam west. He had not understood the man's words, but he understood their meaning.

He dove under an ice floe and went back to his whale companions. But Toozak was not the only human on the bay. A mile away were seamen in whaleboats from the whaling ship *Liberty*. They saw Siku, rowed up to his floe and anchored the boat there. A harpooner was ready to strike Siku when he came up to breathe. The man made no noise as he readied his harpoon and waited. The crew did not talk.

From under the ice, ⌢⌢⌢⌢⌢ could see the wooden bottom of their whaleboat. It lay like a cup on the top of the water. Siku was afraid. He and the others swam farther under the large floe, away from the hunters, pushing up the ice with their huge heads. The ice broke. Air entered the dome. Having breathed, he and the others swam on under the ice floe, miles away from the whalers.

From the surface of the ocean came these words:

"They got away. These whales are smart. They will hide under the ice to avoid us."

Then more words.

"He's not worth the effort, anyway," said the harpooner. "Most of them were small. There's not much blubber on a young whale and the baleen is too short to bother with. Let's go."

He raised the sail of their whaleboat. It filled with wind and the sailors sped back to their whaling ship. ⁓⌇⌇⌇⌇ heard the windlass on the whaling ship whir as the whaleboat was lifted out of the water and put back on its stanchion. ⁓⌇⌇⌇⌇ was about to join ⌇⌇⌇⌇ when from far out in the deeper waters came a deep bass warning call. "_____ ⌇⌇⌇⌇⌇⌇_⌇⌇⌇⌇⌇⌇_____."

Orca whales coming toward you.

⁓⌇⌇⌇⌇ heard the killers skimming his way. He stayed under the ice in the air dome. The orcas reached his floe but would not go under it. Their large black dorsal fins were six feet tall and could snag on the ice if they tried to pursue Siku. The ice whale had the advantage of the ice for protection. The orcas turned away and chased after a group of fat seals. The seals rotated magically, surfaced and swirled off.

When at last Siku heard the orcas chasing seals far out to sea, he swam out from under the ice. The other three spy hopped and, seeing no orcas, hurriedly swam south.

⁓⌇⌇⌇⌇ swam out from under the ice floe only to meet a killer whale, who had been silently waiting for him to leave the floe. Siku turned to swim back under it. The orca grabbed his fluke and bit with crushing pressure. With a powerful thrash of his body, 〜〜〜〜 tore his fluke from the orca's grip, but the predator's strong teeth cut deeply. Quickly the lone killer whale called for another killer whale to come help in his hunt. One arrived. The two circled Siku.

〜〜〜〜 dove down to an ocean valley. He stirred up mud and debris with his flippers and fluke, then swam into the cloudy water. The killer whales pursued but avoided the silt cloud. They circled around it. Minutes passed. 〜〜〜〜 needed to surface for a breath but he did not. He remained down for another half hour. When he finally surfaced, he breathed long and heavy blows. The orcas were gone. Their calls went south. He heard their fading calls moving south. 〜〜〜〜 knew that they had given up on making a meal of him. He blew a great column of air and called out to the other whales.

〜〜〜〜 heard 〜〜〜〜 and swam back to him. He saw that Siku's bleeding fluke would force him to rest. This would slow the group's progress. They must go on and leave Siku behind. He swam back to the group and led the group hurriedly west and then south. It was important to reach the waters of the Bering Sea before the ocean ice froze too thick for them to easily break breathing holes in it.

⌐⌐⌐⌐⌐⌐ swam slowly south, although the orca teeth wound throbbed.

He went on into the Bering Strait, passing by the two Diomede Islands.

Sandhill cranes were flying across the strait, heading south from their nesting grounds in the Siberian wilderness. They were going to Florida and Texas for the winter. Female gray whales swam by him on their way to Baja California, to both give birth and mate. Days later he came to Toozak's old village. Siku was in the Bering Sea, and there he rested.

" \\\\\\\\ _ _ _ _ _ _ ≡ ≡ ≡ ≡ ≡ ≡ _ _ _ \\\\\\\\ ≡ ≡ ≡ ≡ ≡ ≡ _ _ _ \\\\," he whistled joyously. He had found his mother near Saint Lawrence Island.

Also near the island was the whaling ship *Thunder.* The whalers aboard this ship were whaling late in the season. They saw Siku's mother surface and blow, launched a whaleboat, and rowed silently toward her. She was nursing her new daughter and did not hear them. The harpooner sent a harpoon into her body with a line and kegs attached. Then a large exploding bullet was shot from a gun. It slipped through her blubber and into her body cavity. The bomb exploded.

Though wounded, she made no sound, no urgent wail, no shriek of pain.

⎯⌒⌒⌒⌒⌒ swam to her. Her daughter shrilled pitifully as the mother dove, trying to rid herself of the harpoon. It held. The harpooner ran out the line. The kegs attached to it dragged on her. The mother turned and sped directly at the whaleboat. When more whaleboats came to the scene, they attacked her with more harpoons.

She turned away. But the wound in her body was great. More whaleboats appeared above her. Oars dipped from them. The mother swam on. She skimmed the ocean bottom as she rushed toward a rock outcropping to snap the lines. She could not reach it. The lines held her back and she began to drown.

A few minutes later her body rose to the surface. Her breath-plume was red with blood.

Thrashing her flukes in a last spurt of life, she lifted herself out of the water thirty feet, fell back, and drenched the whalers. They hardly noticed. Here was a seventy-ton prize.

The ocean surface quieted down. The waves died into slicks of oil and blood. Jaegers circled overhead. Murres flew around the whalers and guillemots sailed off the sea surface where they had been fishing. The mother was floating.

An ivory gull cried once *"Keeer,"* and soared away.

Milling close to her, ⌇⌇⌇⌇⌇ saw the lines grow taught as his mother was towed by six whaleboats to the *Thunder.* He moaned. His grief was heard through the ocean.

The whalers sang an old whaling song. They stopped singing only long enough to cheer.

The crew rendered the blubber of their last bowhead of the season and poured the oil into barrels. They stored baleen from Siku's mother alongside valuable polar-bear skins in the hold.

⌇⌇⌇⌇⌇ swam in circles around the killing waters. That night he went under an ice floe, made a breathing crack, and hung there. Dawn found him still there.

Feeling the misery of loneliness, he dropped down among the crabs and brittlestars on the ocean floor.

An Arctic octopus, living in a wrecked ship's hull, came out of the captain's quarters and snatched a small fish with the suction cups on her arms. She wrapped it up in them and carried it back to the captain's watery rooms. There she consumed it.

"Ummmmm ummmmmm . . ." ‿⌒⌒⌒⌒ cried. Although he had been weaned from his mother long ago, he grieved that she was gone. In bowhead years, he was still young. His sister, not yet able to get her own food, was adopted by another female. The female suckled her, and after a while milk flowed.

The *Thunder* sailed to a Hawaiian port for the winter. Although the bowhead harvest was declining, these whalers would still be wealthy men.

8

ON THE OCEAN

——— 1871 ———

The Arctic Ocean wreaked its vengeance on the whalers in September of 1871. Forty whaling ships had earlier sailed through the Bering Strait and up the coast of Alaska. Only seven returned. Word had it that the few remaining whales in the Arctic would be coming past Point Barrow in September and they had risked all to get them.

One of those ships, the *Trident*, was captained once again by Thomas Boyd. He was back in the Arctic, this time he had brought his only son, Tom II, with him.

Not far from the ship that day, was 〜〜〜〜 and a small group of ice whales.

The sea was rough and ships were tossing danger-ously. Captain Boyd and the other whaling captains pulled their boats into the calm water between the pack ice and land-fast ice between Icy Cape and Point Franklin. Point Franklin had been named after the Brit-ish explorer who, years later, would be lost attempt-ing to find the Northwest Passage. The crew would wait there for the whales to come south on migration.

As Captain Boyd sailed for Point Franklin, he noticed a whale breaching nearby. It had a mark like an Eskimo dancer on its chin.

"Tom," he called. "It's a whale." Tom II came running.

"Where?" the boy shouted, but there were only whale footprints, an oval swirl of water created by the pumping flukes of a moving whale, and then even those disappeared.

Disappointed, Captain Boyd steered his ship toward the shore.

"We'll wait here," he said. "That wind that's blowing is an easterly one. It will blow the ice pack out to sea, and we can anchor in the deep entrance to the lagoon."

"But the ice seems to be coming closer," Tom II observed.

"Captain Roys taught me about these Arctic winds," said his father. He knew that Arctic winds can be fickle. They will blow north and then switch southwest, toward shore, without warning, pushing any pack ice before it.

An advancing mass of pack ice was to windward and an unforgiving coast was to their lee. At that moment, some lucky ships turned and ran between the great sheet of ice and shore, and sailed southwest toward ice-free waters. Others stayed hoping for the east wind or a sea current to take the pack ice away.

"Father, the ice is closing in!" Tom II cried in alarm.

Captain Boyd ran for the wheel. No sooner had he taken hold of it than he heard the sound of wood splintering. He looked fore and aft. Heavy ice had closed around them.

"The ship!" he cried. "Her stern is stove!"

Glancing toward the other thirty-nine ships strung out in a line, he saw to his horror that many of them were being crushed between shore and the pack ice.

"Abandon ship," Captain Boyd ordered. He turned to Tom II. "Get in the nearest whaleboat. Water is coming in the aft cabin." He departed.

Tom II scrambled to the cabin with the timbers

crackling, put on his winter parka, grabbed his mittens, and ran to a whaleboat. The ship was listing severely to one side.

Tom II swung into the whaleboat. Rowers dropped onto their seats.

"Lower away," he yelled to the men at the stanchion. The whaleboat was lowered onto ice.

"Pull her over the ice to open water!" barked Captain Boyd from the deck. The whalers got out of the whaleboat, stepped onto the ice, grabbed her lines, and pulled with all their might.

The *Trident* listed to one side even more.

"Abandon ship!" Captain Boyd now shouted again. They lowered the four whaleboats, climbed down the ropes and rope ladders, and jumped into them. When every last soul was off the ship, Captain Boyd slid down a rope into the last whaleboat.

The *Trident* was rolling onto her beam ends and splintering under the vise-like grip of the ice. Tom II looked back at her and gasped. In the short time since they had abandoned ship, the *Trident* had been completely crushed by ice. Her sails had collapsed, her beams were splintered. Whale oil was spilling onto the ice, the hold, and into the water.

All the men were straining to pull the whaleboats over the rough ice.

"To seawater," the captain rasped. Suddenly an ice block as big as a house was plowing toward the whaleboat. Tom II grabbed the bench he was sitting on with both hands. His knuckles whitened. The seamen strained and hauled the whaleboat as fast as they could. They finally dragged the boat away from the encroaching ice block and reached ice-free waters. They set the whaleboat afloat, jumped in, and began rowing away from the ice pack.

Other crews from other ships were desperately hauling their whaleboats as well. Seven ships had slipped free of the ice and were out at sea, including the *Daniel Webster*. The crew of the *Trident* drew up alongside her and was welcomed aboard. All seagoing whaling ships rescue other whalers in distress. In fact, helping fellow sailors is the first law of the sea. Packed like sardines, the sailors stood on the *Daniel Webster*'s deck and in the distance watched the *Trident* and other ships splinter into shreds.

Thirty-two ships were abandoned in the ice near Point Belcher, west of Barrow; amazingly no lives were lost, which was not often the case. The Eskimos saw it as the ocean's revenge for killing whales for money instead of for food. Later, the Yankee whalers would refer to it as the Disaster of 1871.

On the *Daniel Webster* Captain Boyd sought out her captain. "This might be the end of whaling," he said to him. "Too few whales, too many wrecks."

"This *is* the end of whaling," the captain answered. "Black oil has been struck in Pennsylvania. It will be cheaper and it keeps on flowing."

Captain Tom Boyd stood on the deck with Tom II and looked out on the windy, gray Arctic Ocean. A lone whale blew. On his chin was a mark shaped like an Eskimo dancer, his hand up, his knees bent.

Despite everything, Tom II smiled. The whale would be safe for now.

The ship turned south to again face the terrible storms of the Bering Sea.

A blustery six weeks later, Captain Boyd and his crew arrived in Hawaii.

Nothing remained of the *Trident.*

9

In the Ocean

———— 1871 ————

~~~~~~~~ *pumped his scarred flukes and* swam by himself behind his group of whales, who were headed southwest for the Russian coast. It was fall.

A pod of beluga whales, white as snow, caught up and followed him. They were stocky and about twice the length of a porpoise. Siku's big wake made swimming easier for them. He also pleased them. He was a gentle whale, a bowhead, and they enjoyed his company. Around them, Arctic lion's mane jellyfish, floated like dream ghosts. Forests of seaweed began to appear below Siku to mark his progress south. The belugas left Siku just beyond Barrow.

Near the Russian coast, ⌇⌇⌇⌇ heard the screeching, lugubrious tones and whistling chatter of other bowhead whale "songs" far ahead of him. It was a comforting sound to a lonely bowhead.

Ahead of him millions of pink salmon hatchlings, the smallest and most northern of the Pacific salmon, were moving in a living cloud. The young salmon were heading for the deep ocean in order to grow. Two years from this time, they would return to the same freshwater streams where they had hatched. There they would spawn, deposit eggs, and die. Their eggs would hatch, the fry would swim downstream to the sea, and the cycle of life and death would go on.

As ⌇⌇⌇⌇ swam south along the Russian coast, he came upon a village. The waters didn't taste right. Dead whales floated around the spot. The scene was morbid. The Yankees were taking only the valuable baleen from the bowheads they were killing now. Whale oil was being replaced by the black fossil oil, so they now killed increasingly just for the baleen.

Siku spy hopped. He saw no people, no dogs, no smoke. The village houses had fallen in; their drying racks were empty.

The walrus and whale population had been decimated. This, together with Yankee diseases like measles, influenza, scarlet fever, and smallpox, had led to starvation and to the collapse of many villages.

The water lapped softly on the shore. Over the swish ⌒⌒⌒⌒⌒⌒ heard the sounds of a whaling ship coming toward him. He dove. The ship was so near that he could hear the men talking on board. Whales listen. He stayed down in the water until he no longer heard them. Then he swam on through the Bering Strait.

10

ON THE LAND

—— 1871 ——

Toozak was hunting caribou on the coast near the Kasegaluk [Ka-SIG-ah-luk] Lagoon seven days travel from his village. Suddenly he heard the shriek of wood splintering in the distance. He knew that sound. Ice was crushing the white man's wooden whaling ships. He climbed an ice block and squinted. Seamen were strung out across the ice hauling whaleboats. Their ships were crushed to splinters between the pack ice and land-fast ice. He smiled; they were leaving their ships too fast to take the furnishings. There would be splendid articles to salvage later from the wrecked ships.

When he got home, Toozak found his father-in-law

insulating his house with snow. He piled snow around the walls, sealed one more wind leak as the young man was getting off his sled.

"Kakinnaaq," Toozak said. "The white men are abandoning ships that are caught in the ice. They are taking only their lives. Let us get their furnishings."

"We must see what they left behind. Get my big sleds," Kakinnaaq said, smiling. "We go."

Toozak harnessed six dogs to each of two sleds. Kakinnaaq took one, he the other, and they mushed for a week over new-fallen snow to the ships that were heaved over in the ice.

Toozak and Kakinnaaq climbed carefully onto the tilted deck of a ship and stepped around broken rigging, spilled oil, and the bricks of the broken tryworks.

"Pass things to me," said Kakinnaaq. "I will put them on the sleds. I see inland Eskimos coming for the salvage. We must hurry."

Toozak passed pots, pans, knives, line, and even the huge windlass to Kakinnaaq. When they had loaded all they could carry, they lashed down the load and rode off. Toozak was in the lead, laughing victoriously and looking back at his wife's father. Suddenly he stopped laughing. A whiskey cask was lying under a coil of line on Kakinnaaq's sled. He halted the dogs. Walking back to his father-in-law's sled, he grabbed the box and threw it off the sled.

"What are you doing?" Kakinnaaq shouted, jumping off his sled to pick up the whiskey cask.

"You know it's poison. You can't hunt when you drink!" Toozak's eyes misted as he realized what he'd done. He had spoken disrespectfully to an elder, an evil thing.

"You're right," Kakinnaaq said gruffly to Toozak, and got back on the rear of his sled. He placed the cask on the snow. *"Kiita, kiita."* The dogs started off again.

Toozak wondered if the curse from his boyhood was finally catching up with him. The world was changing—the whales becoming fewer and fewer, the walrus disappearing. Yankees would trade whiskey to locals for furs and information about the whereabouts of whales. Then they would hunt the whales, taking only the baleen and leaving the rest of the animal to rot. And the hunters who drank wouldn't care. Toozak knew that alcohol must be an evil thing if it allowed people simply to stop caring about the land and the animals. Soon, there wouldn't be any whales left at all, and who would be around to care?

Toozak knew that he would always care. It was his mission—his destiny—to protect Siku from harm.

II

ON THE LAND

——— 1918 ———

For two generations, the number of bowhead whales in the Arctic Ocean remained very small. Although Siku was spotted once by an Eskimo whaler in 1885, no one had seen him since. From time to time over the years, Toozak's grandson, Toozak III, and his grandson's son, Toozak IV, paddled out in the ocean to look for Siku and then paddled back unrewarded.

Toozak IV made his home in Wainwright, an Inupiat Eskimo village, that was a center for whaling. Like many Eskimos, the Toozaks had begun to wonder about the powers of shamans, but they each told their sons of the curse and the promise to protect Siku. Theirs was a history book handed down by voice. They had no written language. Toozak IV had come to Wainwright for work and because he still believed Siku was alive and that he must protect him.

When Toozak IV's wife, Lilaaq, gave birth to Charlie Toozak V, the market for bowhead baleen had vanished, and Yankee whaling abruptly ended. Yankees were no longer sailing the Arctic waters to hunt the whale. Only the fur traders remained. They had married Eskimo women and stayed on in the Arctic operating the fur trading posts, and fishing and hunting for their families.

Then Wainwrighters reported sighting an increasing number of whales swimming by their village. They were thrilled. A whale would help feed many townsfolk all year. Gathering a whaling crew together, they set up a whale camp fifteen miles out on the sea ice. It consisted of two white canvas tents—one a sleeping tent, the other a cooking tent, and a sealskin boat with willow ribs. They propped the aft end of the boat on a block of ice at the water's edge so that they could slide it into the water at a moment's notice. They watched and waited.

When Toozak III heard about it, he and his son went out on the sea ice to work for the whaling crew. They cleaned pots and pans and did some cooking. They watched the black water for whales. These two searched for one whale in particular—the one they had only heard stories of, with the mark of the dancing Eskimo on its chin.

Spring passed to summer. One morning Toozak IV was on foot when he saw on the ocean a smoke-belching ship. It had no sails, but it moved steadily along and was throwing something into the water. That afternoon he found a massive fishnet on the beach by the camp.

"Aapa," he said to his father. "I've heard that whales get tangled in these Yankee nets."

Together, they walked to the beach and gazed at the yards and yards of net and ropes. Toozak III held his son's hand as the boy leaned out as far as he could and grabbed the net. Together they pulled it high onto the beach.

Before them a stream of mist shot into the air and a whale breached. On his chin was the image of an Eskimo dancer!

"Siku!" father and son gasped. The whale looked at them and they at him. A spark ignited between them, and then the great whale rolled on his side and slid gracefully back into the water. When he was out of sight, Toozak III and Toozak IV looked at each other in great surprise.

"That is the great Siku," said Toozak III. He is still alive. It is a good thing we pulled the net from the water. Nets like that are dangerous to him and all whales."

That winter the flu came to the Eskimos in the village near Wainwright. Many died. Among them was Lilaaq, Toozak IV's wife.

Toozak IV laid her coffin, along with hundreds of others, on the frozen ground in the cemetery. She and the other dead could not easily be buried until the June thaw.

"I have no life here without Lilaaq. I know what I must do," Toozak IV said. "I must find the old whaling captain who lives in Barrow. He is a generous man, and knows many things. He can teach me about whales and the old ways. They say he is called Ernest, and he knows more about ice whales than anyone. My life is now Siku's."

They walked slowly home from the cemetery, gathered food, weapons, and a stack of furs as well as pots and pans.

"I must go with you," Toozak III said to Toozak IV. "We must protect Siku together. There are new threats to him. We will learn to find whales and how to think like them from one of the great whaling captains. One who knows them in the old ways. Our life here is over."

He counted on his fingers and said, "Siku is seventy years old. He is very old and we must continue to protect him."

It did not take the family long to gather their possessions. Harnessing the dog team to a sled, Toozak IV stood beside his father at the rear of the graceful carrier. His son, Charlie, was nestled in the sled basket among caribou furs.

Toozak IV raised his voice. *"Kiita!"* he shouted. The dogs bolted out of the village. Charlie giggled.

Three days later, they rode into prosperous Barrow with its trading post, community house, grammar school, and restaurant.

Wooden houses clustered on wide streets. Caribou antlers were scattered aomng them and hides hung on stretchers before them. Snowdrifts were still unmelted against many houses and old whale bones marked the community house.

Toozak III and IV were pleased. They could be happy here. That afternoon they rode to the western end of town and unpacked.

Days later, Toozak IV started building a sod hut with whale bones that he had found on the beach for supports. He next got a job at the store and he and the small family settled in with help from the women in the village.

When the eiders were flying over Barrow in black threads five miles long, Toozak IV knew that it was time to approach Ernest, the famous Eskimo whaling captain.

He came upon him standing beside his sealskin *umiaq* at the edge of the land-fast ice looking out to sea. He had his back to the village and was smiling at a cloud with a dark gray bottom on the horizon.

"Water sky," he said as Toozak IV came up beside him.

"Water throws dark shadows on the bottom of clouds. Snow and ice throw white ones. So the dark bottom of clouds say 'open water.' It's called *uiñiq* [UN-yik] a 'lead.' We go whaling when we see the water sky. It means the whales are migrating past, even though we don't see many whales anymore. Yankee whaling nearly wiped them out."

"I know of one whale," Toozak IV said. "I call him Siku. He is still out there. I saw him in a place far away from here. Teach me where the whales swim on their migration so that I may find him again."

Ernest turned and looked silently at Toozak IV before he spoke.

"Why must you find him?"

"My ancestors said a Toozak must protect him . . . I am a Toozak. I must honor this."

"And why is that?"

"The first Toozak showed some Yankee whalers where a group of ice whales lay. He didn't think about the harm that would come to them."

"That was very wrong," Ernest said in a quiet voice.

"They slaughtered them all. A great darkness was upon us," Toozak IV said, his head down. "My family's stories of this tragedy have been passed down for generations by word of mouth. My father told me."

Ernest glanced at the miles of white sea ice before them.

"But Siku lives. That sounds like a good omen. Maybe his spirit will end some of the Yankee evils." He squinted toward the north. "The Yankees' Bureau of Indian Affairs makes our schoolchildren speak only English, not our own language. They must speak English from the moment they enter the school building until the time they leave at the end of the day. They are hit with a ruler if they speak Inupiat. That's not right."

"No, it's not," said Toozak IV. "I fear that will happen to my own son. I don't want to lose him."

Ernest nodded.

"He will be sent out of Barrow to some faraway place for high school. We have none here. Know this so that when the time comes, you can decide what you want to do. But this news of Siku is good news. This Siku must be a good spirit. I will show you where the whales swim on their way to the Beaufort Sea."

The next day Ernest and Toozak IV pulled Ernest's *umiaq* on a sled across the land-fast ice to the watery lead and set the *umiaq* afloat. Beautifully crafted, the boat with its wooden frame was covered with sealskins. The skins had been sewn together in the traditional way by Ernest's wife and her women friends, and would not leak. Their work sat like a piece of art on the water.

The two stepped into the *umiaq*.

Quietly they paddled on the glittering water. Diamond snow sparkled in the air.

When they were almost a mile out, Ernest tapped Toozak IV on the shoulder and pointed to swirling eddies on the surface of the ocean.

"*Kala*—whale footprints," he said happily. "One has passed here."

Toozak IV looked at them.

They paddled farther on the calm ocean. They could not find the whale.

12

ON THE LAND

— 1946 —

"You are a Christian," the minister said to Charlie Toozak V, now a young man in his late twenties, as he sprinkled him with holy water and murmured a prayer.

"I will use your English name. I will call you Charlie." The minister then shook his hand. Charlie Toozak was the first Eskimo of his family to have two names, English and Eskimo. "Welcome to the fold."

With this deed, Charlie thought the shaman's curse that he had heard about from his father and grandfather would vanish. But outside the church he still heard generations of voices repeating the words in his head: "Protect Siku until he dies." But then, for the first time, he thought he heard an echo of those words: "Or until he saves a Toozak."

That's odd, he thought. *Imagine a whale saving a person. Those shamans are pretty clever.* He pushed back his hood and ran his fingers through his hair. Try as he might to brush it away, the curse was still upon him like snowfall. But now he had something new to think about. He could not shake it even though he no longer believed in shamans.

"Oh, the power of Eskimo stories," he lamented.

It was a new time, and yet the curse held him.

Several days later, U.S. Navy freight planes landed on the Barrow airstrip. Barges were being unloaded at the beach. Charlie Toozak went to see them. Sailors were unloading building supplies, vehicles, and machinery. An officer beside him said the materials had been transported here to build an Arctic research lab for the navy. When it was finished it would contain dining rooms, business offices, laboratories, and living quarters for officers. Others would be for biologists, hydrographers, weather scientists, oceanographers, and anthropologists.

While Charlie was staring at the wondrous materials being loaded onto huge trucks, the officer at his elbow told him that the United States had just ended a war. Now scientists wanted to know more about the people, plants, animals, marine life, and ocean currents in the Arctic.

"They are hiring," he said. "You should look into it."

The next day Charlie Toozak applied for a job and was later hired to help with the wolf research program. A dozen captive wolves were being studied to learn how to survive the Arctic winters without water. He talked to his charges with howls and gestures and comforted them when they were ill. He loved his work and was good at it.

At the lab he spoke English and rarely used his Eskimo language. One day when his father asked him a question, he answered in English.

That day Toozak IV said to himself, *I cannot speak to my son. I cannot ask him where the airplanes come from, or how the trucks move without dogs. Have I lost him?*

13

ON THE LAND

——— 1948 ———

I n the summer of 1948, a freight ship sailed through the Bering Strait and north on the Arctic Ocean. Belching black clouds, its propellers cutting the water, it steamed on to Barrow in only three days instead of weeks.

"Haul the crates out of the hold," ordered Captain Tom Boyd IV. "We are at Barrow, Alaska." His thirteen-year-old son, Thomas Boyd V, know as Tommy, was watching the sun dip halfway below the horizon and rise again. The summer was nearly over. They must get out of the Arctic. Then, out of the ocean nearby, came a rare sight, a bowhead whale. It blew, breached, and dove.

Tommy stared.

"Dad," he said, "I just saw a whale. He had a funny white spot on his chin."

"Say that again, Tommy."

"A whale. He had a spot that looks like a man dancing on his chin."

"Really?" his dad questioned as he stared out into the ocean. Just then, the whale spy hopped out of the ocean, greeting the ship. Captain Boyd sucked in his breath and stood motionless until the whale disappeared back into the ocean, leaving waves in its wake. "There is a story our ancestors tell about seeing a whale just like that years ago. Could it be that same one with the mark on its chin? If so, it's got to be a hundred years old! I didn't even think there were any bowheads left around here."

Tommy's eyes widened. His father continued speaking. "Whaling used to be a very important industry around here. You know all of your forefathers—my grandfather, and his father before him, for as long back as we know—worked on the sea. And some of them worked in the whaling industry. It employed thousands of skilled crews to harvest the whales. But the commercial whalers depleted the oceans and now there just aren't many whales left. So whaling isn't a business here anymore."

"But Eskimos kill whales," Tommy protested.

"Yes, but for thousands of years, they only killed what they needed. The whales are food and life's necessities."

He patted his son on the back. "Maybe the whales are coming back." He gazed out to the ocean once more and walked over to the railing to see that the cargo was unloaded with care.

14

IN THE OCEAN

——— 1948 ———

Near the village of Barrow, pulsating mechanical booms shook ⌒⌒⌒⌒⌒'s ocean space. He surfaced and spy hopped. A group of men were setting off dynamite on the ice. They were looking for oil—not whale oil but petroleum. The roar of the engines bothered his ears and body. Taking a breath, he dove deep into the cold, clear water. Swimming as rapidly as he was able to, he put distance between himself and the explosions. When he met the coastal current, he slowed down. The ocean currents split at Point Barrow. One flowed strong as a river to the north through heavy ice. The other flowed east along the Canadian coast.

Every year since he had been born, Siku had taken the coastal current, but not this time. This time the blasts forced him to take a more difficult route farther north through broken ice to get to his summer home. Enjoying the tumbling floes as he swam, he finally caught up with a group of male bowheads.

They had more members than they'd had in the last fifty years. No Yankees had been whaling since then. Now the ice whales were increasing in numbers—coming out of hiding in bays and remote waters. ∿∿∿∿∿ was among them.

∿∿∿∿∿ swam quietly, listening to the male bowheads and the whistles and roars of the females ahead of them. The females were communicating with each other and their newborns. Swimming among the ice chunks on the northern current, he heard no more whaling ships.

Then ∿∿∿∿∿ heard the distinctive sound of *umiaq* paddles. He noted the location of the *umiaq* and turned away.

A harpooner in the *umiaq* saw ᔊᔊᔊᔊ turn and tossed the harpoon.

Siku threw himself thirty feet in the air. When he splashed back down into the water, the waves swamped the *umiaq*. Siku would not give himself to this crew. He did not know them.

He was now one hundred years old and weighed sixty-five tons, and he could rock a whaling boat with a single swing of his huge flukes. He rose again, and thrust himself out of the sea. Water rained down. The great splash reflected the sun's rays, creating a glittering orange, green, and yellow waterfall. It was a beautiful moment. The huge wave that followed lifted the boat and drove it toward an ice floe.

Other boats came to help, thinking he was dead. But he was not dead. Pumping his gigantic fluke, he dove.

ᔊᔊᔊᔊ swam under the *umiaqs*. The whalers watched the great whale in awe as he disappeared beneath the ice. They knew this whale was special.

A living mat of sea life growing on the seafloor glowed green, red, and brown. He slowed down and lolled until he heard the whalers' paddles in the water. With that, he plunged down into the depths of Barrow Canyon.

In its dark valley he rested for almost forty-five minutes before rising to breathe. The whalers had left. Soaked by ～～～～～ 's splash, they had paddled to their ice camp to get out of their freezing, wet parkas.

～～～～～ surfaced. Arctic cod circled him in a Ferris wheel of fish wizardry. They were seeking the same tiny food that he sought.

～～～～～ felt emboldened by the many whirling cod. He spy hopped to see where he was. He saw only guillemots, in their black plumage, their heads held high. He saw no whalers.

～～～～～ lay on the surface of the water breathing heavily. His rostrum protruded slightly. Slowly he became aware of a new sensation . . . a warm current. Barely a fluke wide, it flowed over him like a scarf. It had come from the faraway Atlantic Ocean. Was it a sign of changes to come to the Arctic?

Siku swam directly toward the Beaufort Sea. Even though he had strayed from the familiar route, magnetic fields told him where to go. Despite his one hundred years, the deep grooves in his brain still processed data from the sun, water, and weather and reported it to his body. He knew the sea and all its voices.

Along the coast, ~∿∿∿∿ felt that thread of warm water again and swam with it until it was gone. Windblown whitecaps took its place.

Steadily ~∿∿∿∿ swam slowly on, heading northeast to the summer feeding grounds.

15

ON THE LAND

——— 1959 ———

Something *good happened on January 3, 1959.* Alaska became the United States of America's forty-ninth state. The people of Barrow celebrated.

Charlie Toozak did a one-arm handstand and a high kick that Ernest had taught him so long ago when his father had sought out the great whaler. They were both games in the Eskimo Olympics, and he was good at them. Ernest cheered for him.

"Aarigaa!" people shouted at the end of the performance.

Charlie's wife, Maria, and her women friends were singing happily as they prepared precious whale for everyone.

That summer, Charlie's son, Robert Toozak (Toozak VI) and his friend Benny (Ernest's grandson) were paddling a large kayak not far from shore when they saw something odd—an exploratory commercial crabber from the Bering Sea.

"They're setting crab pots," said Benny. "Let's go see them."

The commercial fishermen warned them off. They were casting huge pots into the sea in hopes of finding new crabbing grounds and didn't want the native people to watch them too closely. As the pots sank the men fed out over two hundred feet of rope. Bobbing buoys marked the pots.

Eii, murmured Robert to himself. *I'll come back and cut the ropes when no one is around.* Even though his father claimed not to believe in it, he too had passed down to his son the stories of the family legend and their mission to protect the special whale, Siku, and whales in general. Robert knew these ropes would be a danger to the whale, and he leaped at the chance to protect him, as seven generations of his family had done, and to cause some mischief.

That night, Robert would cut the ropes, much to the outrage of the fishermen. He continued to look out for Siku's safety, though he never saw the whale.

In 1964, Robert Toozak married a woman named Flossie and, a year later, his first child, a girl named Emily Toozak, was born.

16

ON THE LAND

—— 1980 ——

On a day in late May of the year 1980, Emily Toozak, now fifteen, and her younger brother, Oliver Toozak VII, were sitting on the bluff behind their house. A white cloud with a dark bottom was visible on the horizon.

"Water sky," Emily Toozak said. "It says that the leads are open, those rivers of water in the sea ice. The whales migrate up these ocean lanes to the Beaufort Sea." She pulled her hood closer to protect her face from the wind. It held her warm breath like a heater. Emily loved to hear stories of her grandfather's teacher, Ernest. Very old now, he had been a great whaler, and knew more about whales than anyone else in Barrow. He lived in the last sod house in Barrow, and used his knowledge of nature to track the whales. He had even helped her great-grandfather protect them.

"*Eii,*" she said. "Water sky. The leads are open. Many whales are going past. I know it is dangerous but I am going to walk out on the land-fast ice as far as I can and stand under the water sky. I want to see the whales going by." She did not tell Oliver how many times she had already done this by herself, hoping to catch a glimpse of a whale. Unlike her younger brother, she *did* believe in the old ways, and knew she must do everything she could to watch over the whales and their spirits.

"Okay," Oliver said. Normally he grumbled when he had to accompany Emily on adventures. He was not interested in the old ways at all. But he was in a good mood today. The two scrambled over white ice blocks with their blue-green shadows until they came to a pressure ridge, the hard, land-fast ice that the pack ice from the north hits and pushes up into mountains. They picked their way up and climbed to the top. There they looked out over the ocean.

Just then, in the cobalt black lead below them, the water parted and the rostrum of a whale emerged. He breathed out, sending up a fountain of mist. It turned to ice fog and fell back into the water. There was a pause, then a huge bowhead whale breached. He rose almost eye level with them. On his lip was a white patch shaped like a dancing Eskimo.

The two siblings gasped. The whale was so close. He was huge.

Both children had heard the story of the curse put on their ancestors, though neither of them really believed in curses. But suddenly Emily felt she understood the bond the first Toozak had felt for the whale. "It's Siku," she whispered. "Great Whale, I will always protect you."

Oliver laughed. "That's impossible. How could you protect him? He's too big. Even his flukes would get in the way."

"Jonah was saved by a whale," said Emily. "Maybe Siku could save me."

"From what?" Oliver scoffed.

Emily took in another long look at the whale. Before Oliver could inquire any further, she said, "Let's get closer." They climbed down the pressure ridge to the turquoise shelf of ice at the water's edge. On the shelf ice, Emily, with the wind screaming around her, tapped Oliver's arm and pointed.

"Oliver, look in the distance," she said. "An icebreaker."

"So what? No bowhead would ever get near a boat. Let's go home," he said. "I'm cold."

"We have to stay! We're Toozaks. I want to watch. I want to see that whale again. Siku could be in danger!"

"You can stay, but I'm going home." He climbed back up the way they had come, and then descended out of sight.

Emily Toozak stared at the distant icebreaker, wondering how to protect Siku from this. She searched the blue-purple lead of open water for him.

Siku suddenly breached not fifty feet from her. He turned and looked Emily Toozak in the eyes. Emily looked back at him.

"GO! GO! SIKU, GO!" she shouted, and the great whale splashed back in the water. The droplets rose as high as her head. Emily saw big footprints heading north.

But then the footprints turned around and came back toward her. Siku swam up to the ice edge and rolled onto his side, bringing an eye to the surface. He peered up at Emily Toozak. A flash of recognition passed between them.

"I will protect you," she whispered, and touched her cheek.

Siku dove, and waved his fluke. Emily Toozak was transfixed. The whale lingered as if he was glad to see her.

There must be something about me, she reasoned, *that runs through to me from all of my ancestors because I feel like Siku knows me.*

Siku dove out of sight. The icebreaker turned and steamed east.

The water sky was gone. The ice had closed in, freezing and covering the lead.

Emily Toozak stood quietly, enchanted by Siku's white-and-blue world. Finally she climbed up the pressure ridge to the flat ice, then descended and walked back to the general store. Inside, she took off her parka and sat down at a table. Oliver was not there, as she thought he might be, only Ernest's grandson, Benny. Benny was her father's best friend. When he saw her he got another cup of coffee and came across the room with the two cups and sat down at her table. Emily Toozak pulled her chair closer and thanked him for the coffee. Benny was, like his grandfather, one of the best whaling captains on the North Slope. He knew the old ways. He would know if what she had seen had been real.

"I saw a whale today," she said. "I think it was Siku."

"Aarigaa!" said Benny. "The whales are slowly coming back since only Eskimos can hunt them now. And they only give themselves to so few."

Benny sipped his coffee, looking at Emily Toozak thoughtfully. "Siku?" he questioned.

Emily Toozak looked long at Benny. She straightened

her back. "I have heard about him my whole life. But I saw him today for the first time. He spoke to me." She broke off, embarrassed. "Well, he didn't really speak. But something happened between us. I can't really say. I have to find Siku again," she said. "He is not far from here. Will you take me out on the water?"

Although she believed that shamans were just men who made up things, she was beginning to believe that there was a shred of truth about that curse her grandfather had gone on about. "Maybe it's not a curse . . . maybe it's a kind of bond."

Benny looked at her face deeply. "You really want to find him?" Emily nodded. "And then what?" he asked. She shrugged.

"All right," he said, "I will take you. But it's dangerous at sea. We will need to wait until the ice breaks up in July."

Emily Toozak smiled.

17

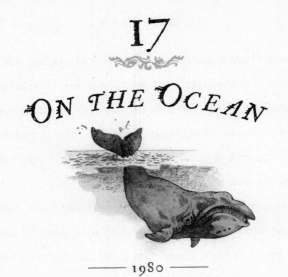

ON THE OCEAN

1980

"It's a good day to travel," Benny said, when Emily saw him on the beach.

"Lets go find Siku."

"We can use my *umiaq*," he said.

"And I will bring my brother," she said. "He will want to come too." She went to find Oliver all the while thinking of Siku. She returned with him, trying to make him excited at the thought of going out on the water.

"Why don't you get yourself a real boat, Benny?" Oliver asked.

Benny laughed. "A real boat? Skin boats are still the best for the ice. You can't get anything better; they're light, flexible, tough, paddle well, sail well, and you can fix them anywhere."

Benny put on a white parka and pants that made him partially invisible to the whales. It was July and the sea ice was breaking up and scattering. While Benny steadied the skin boat, Oliver climbed into the bow. He had brought his seal harpoon and rifle. He tucked them under his arm.

"You are not hurting Siku," Emily Toozak said when she saw what Oliver had brought along.

"Don't worry, Emily!" said Oliver. "See this little harpoon? I am hunting seals, not whales."

"But Siku may see it and think we are hunting him," Emily said.

She got in last, grabbed a paddle and seated herself firmly, as if to say *I am Emily Toozak, the seventh generation of Toozaks. I am here to find Siku and protect him from all who would harm him. It is my responsibility, the responsibility of my family.* They soundlessly launched the graceful *umiaq*.

She dug in her paddle.

"Let's go," Benny said softly. They dug in, and the skin boat skimmed through the water. It glided past floes of turquoise-blue ice as it silently parted the water. Murres looped around the paddlers, got back on track, and flew on to their breeding grounds.

Oliver spotted a seal hauled out on an ice floe. He pointed and Benny turned the boat in that direction. Then a plume shot up thirty feet above the sea surface.

"There," whispered Benny. He refrained from pointing to the whale. Old whalers believe pointing was an insult to the whale.

Siku had been in these waters overnight. Now he spy hopped, saw the boat, and dove. The three people put down their paddles. Oliver stood in the bow waiting for the whale to surface again. Emily Toozak sat stone-still. They were silent. Fifteen minutes passed. Then Siku's rostrum surfaced nearby. A plume of warm breath rose from the ocean's surface. The whale seemed skittish.

"He thinks we're hunting him," whispered Oliver, putting down his seal harpoon.

"But we're not," Emily said firmly but quietly.

"He doesn't know that," said Oliver.

Siku was alarmed. He dove and then surfaced next

to the skin boat. The seal harpoon and line went overboard. Siku's fluke caught in the line and he tugged the boat seaward. Emily's first thought was for the whale. *I must do something to help him*. He dove deeper and came up again, tangling the rope around him more tightly.

Emily quickly drew her knife from her belt, reached down, and started to cut the lines. The boat rocked. She leaned over the side, her knife still in her hand. Siku was almost free. But the rope was caught around the narrows of his fluke. He pumped his flukes to cast off the rope but could not. He breached and fell backward. The spray soared fifty feet high and fell back, drenching them, nearly washing them over the side. Benny was on his knees trying to steady the boat. Emily was practically over the side, slashing wildly at the remaining ropes. She would not give up.

The whale tried to rise in the water, to see the girl whose eyes he had looked into just yesterday. But he was caught.

18

IN THE OCEAN

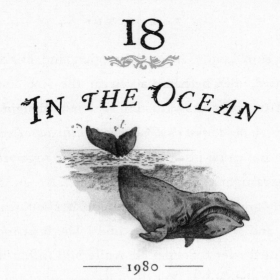

—— 1980 ——

~~~~~~ *swam down toward the brittlestar-dotted* ocean floor. The girl in the skin boat had cut him almost free, but the line was still entangled around his fluke. He swam to the underside of a large ice floe.

Once there, he stopped. He found a natural crack and hung in it, breathing heavily. Arctic cod, small fish with brown backs and purplish sides, darted past him. A seal slid into the water from the floe. She caught a cod then climbed back up to the floe.

Siku thrashed his flukes. The rope still held. He swam around and around the underwater bottom of the ice floe. The rope grew tight. He needed one more pull when he heard a voice.

"A paddle! Hand me a paddle!" It was the girl. She had fallen out of the skin boat onto the ice when she had leaned out to cut him free. Getting quickly to her feet, she tried to reach for the paddle just as an ice block broke off from the large floe. Swiftly it was carried farther out to sea with her on it.

"A line!" she screamed. "Throw me a line." Benny paddled hard, but the current was too swift. Ice floes were thick around the *umiaq*. There was nothing he could do in such dangerous waters and powerful currents.

Emily Toozak was carried farther down the coast to the east.

"Benny! Oliver! Help!"

Siku hung in his air pocket under Emily Toozak's ice floe. He kept working the muscles that power his flukes and at last the rope fell away. The ice moved with him. He suffered burns from the rope. Still, he did not leave.

Siku, underneath the terrified girl, guided the huge floe east toward Smith Bay. He sighed at the under-water smell of it. Each fall he had fed on the abundant plankton near there. The girl with the kind eyes spoke out loud.

“I tried to take the rope off you, Siku. Now I am lost.”

“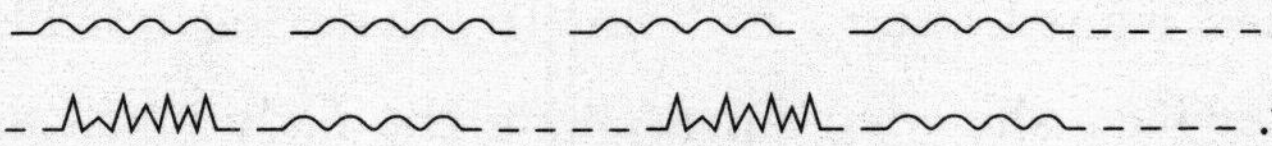.”

a whale shrilled, calling him to the Eastern Beaufort Sea.

Siku did not answer.

19

IN THE OCEAN

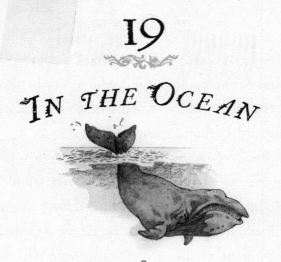

——— 1980 ———

Word was radioed all over town that Emily Toozak had been lost on an ice floe. Almost immediately four members of the Sea and Land Rescue Team got back into Benny's *umiaq* and paddled to the east after Emily. The paddlers were volunteers in the dangerous work of rescuing people in this unforgiving land. They were strong and adventurous young men and women.

Benny took his seat in the stern and called out a fast paddling stroke. The crew caught the rhythm and the boat sped forward. By the time they reached the ice from which Emily Toozak's floe had broken off, she was nowhere to be seen. The currents split here and Benny could not tell which way her floe had gone. Had they taken her north into the pack ice or east toward Canada?

He decided he needed more than this boat to determine which direction the currents had taken her. He returned to the trading post, hopped onto his snow machine, and sped to the Arctic Research Lab for help. Some of the rescue team came with him.

It took valuable time for him to explain that Emily Toozak was lost at sea and that a boat with a stronger motor than his was needed. It took another fifteen minutes to ready a power boat for the water. Once they were afloat, Benny, the rescue volunteers, and the navy men motored out beyond the point then east. Emily Toozak was nowhere to be found. The naval officer in charge said she might be dead. He motored back to the Arctic Research Lab while rescue workers continued to hunt. Someone from the lab had contacted Wayne Airlines, and their planes were now flying overhead.

But Benny knew Emily Toozak was still alive and that he would find her. This time he took his kayak.

He would search the eastward-flowing current and the coves and river deltas along its way. He paddled alone.

The freight airplanes passed overhead, and a search helicopter circled. A modern ship passed him carrying supplies for the oil fields. Its crewmen had been alerted to watch for a girl on an ice floe. They lined the deck, and several waved at Benny. He did not wave back.

"I wouldn't be so worried," Benny said to the Arctic world of ice, clouds, wind, and green water, "if only Emily Toozak had been raised in the traditional Eskimo ways. Then she would know how to survive. Her generation isn't as skilled in Eskimo wisdom." Benny was one of the only ones of his generation left who knew how to survive in the wilderness with little but a knife.

Common eiders were still flying in flocks headed east toward the shoreline in order to obtain the driftwood, grasses, and reeds they needed to build nests and raise their young. Terns circled overhead and flew toward the gravel beaches where they make their nests. The birds said, "Summer is here." But there were no bird clues to say where the current had taken Emily Toozak.

As he paddled Benny felt that there was something about this girl and Siku. Both, he knew instinctively, were alive. Emily Toozak's ice floe had grounded somewhere. Siku, Benny assumed, was unharmed and had gone on to the Eastern Beaufort Sea.

Thinking the current might have carried her to Cape Simpson, he paddled toward it. He was gone three days. His food was sun-dried caribou and fish. He carried freshwater.

The sea was calm and he could paddle steadily. At last he saw bits of mosses and sticks floating on the water. They told him he was approaching the cape.

A fish surfaced nearby. He did not stop to catch it but paddled on. Others might have used an outboard or powerboat, but Benny was from the old school and preferred to travel on his own power.

At the cape, he stopped. The cape was still blocked with ice that swirled and tumbled; it was still early summer and thousand of ice floes freckled the sea.

Away from the large floes, Benny rested. The sun sank slightly toward the horizon and then rose. The long two-month day was upon this world. He watched the sky and ocean turn bright green then yellow gold. He sat still in admiration, but knew he had to paddle the long way back to Barrow.

Robert Toozak and Flossie were at the trading post waiting for him. They walked slowly down the beach when he arrived, afraid to hear the news. Benny stepped out of his kayak shaking his head.

20

ON THE LAND

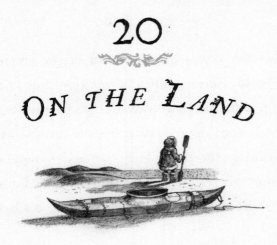

——— 1980 ———

Hours passed. Emily Toozak lay still and cold on the ice floe. Silently, Siku stayed with her and was pushing her and the ice floe with his rostrum. It rode up on a shoal near the beach and crunched to a stop.

The jolt woke Emily. She saw she was grounded, ran to the edge of the floe, and excitedly jumped off. Frightened but glad to be on land, she instantly wondered where she was. The land around the bay looked like the land around Barrow, but she knew it could be almost anyplace on the north coast of Alaska.

Whoosh! She heard the unmistakable sound of a whale

blow. The whale was near the shore. Rising to her toes, she rubbed her eyes and stared.

Another whoosh, then another and four more. Fountains of mist rose and drifted away. There were many whales here. Emily Toozak ran down to the beach to watch them.

One of them breached, fell over backward, and, after a monumental splash, raised his fluke. Then he lifted his head out of the water. There was a white mark on his chin—the dancing Eskimo.

"Siku! You are Siku," she shouted, clapped her hands, and ran down to the water's edge to watch him. His eighty-ton body was as graceful as the small ivory gull above her. She smiled and wrote *Siku* in the gravelly beach as if the word would hold him there.

Then Emily Toozak halted. Looking out at the dark shape in the water, she realized the impossible truth. Siku had pushed her ice floe to land.

"Thank you!" she called out, her voice shaky and rough. Tears welled up in her eyes. Siku had saved her life.

As she turned her back, her Arctic instincts took over. Snuggling her parka hood up against her face, she closed her eyes to better think what to do, then opened them and drew a deep breath.

I hope I run into a hunter or traveler, she thought.

Walking up the beach, she waved good-bye to Siku as she reached the tundra and began searching the thawing landscape for a sign of human life. Grasses and lichens rolled out to the horizon. Wildflowers were just beginning to bloom. The scene was a beige-and-white carpet reaching to the very curve of the earth. She could not walk that endless space without food. How would she get it?

Water was no problem. The land had hundreds of thawing freshwater ponds whose water was drinkable. The problem was food.

Emily Toozak climbed a frost heave, a bump of land raised into a hill by the freeze, and tried to locate a village. Instead of a village, she saw the wreckage of an old schooner tossed up on the bay's beach. It was all that was left of some white men's attempt to get through the Northwest Passage.

The schooner lay on its side, its wave-battered deck standing almost vertical. Emily Toozak scrambled over ice blocks and black beach stones to get to it. She grabbed the broken deck boards and climbed to a door. Peering through it, she saw the ship's galley. It too was tipped on its side and empty.

"Salvaged," she said, disappointed. "They must have taken

everything when they abandoned ship." Then, thinking that the ship's crew might have drowned in the icy waters, she had another thought. *Or did my people find the ship and take everything? I hope so. That might mean I am not too far from a village. But where?*

Deciding to hunt for some overlooked scrap of food in spite of the bareness of the ship, she teetered onto one of its walls, now a floor.

"Pilot-bread crackers, cans of some kind of meat, beans, anything would be great." She picked her way around the ruins of the kitchen and into the pantry.

Empty.

Her heart sank. In discouragement, she flopped down on a battered mattress. Beside it was a ripped blanket. Getting quickly to her feet, she dragged them both to the vertical deck and tossed them down to the beach below. A cooking kit rolled out of the blanket onto the sand.

"Good," she said. "I can cook . . . if I had matches."

Her brow furrowed.

"How did my ancestors make fire? I'm sure I've been told. Think, think, think." She clambered over the wreck and climbed down to the mattress.

With the blanket she made a shelter by tying it to

some broken boards on the ship and pulling the mattress under it, just in case any summer snowstorms should come.

"Maybe a plane will fly by from the oil fields . . . but how do I signal it? Maybe I could use the blanket as a flag."

Whoosh. Emily Toozak turned. A great whale was swimming slowly through the clear icy water. He was feeding in the bay.

"I wish I ate plankton," she sighed. "Hey, maybe I can— but I'll get wet trying. That idea's no good."

"You are good company," she called to Siku.

He thrust up his rostrum, blew mist, and disappeared.

Exhausted and discouraged, Emily Toozak lay down on her mattress and instantly fell asleep.

When Emily awoke hours later, the tide was out. Although there is only a small difference between high and low tide in this part of the world, a high tide had brought some rare kelp to her beach from somewhere nearby. Torn from its moorings by a storm, riding the waves and swells, it had been deposited on the beach by the low tide.

"I must be nearer to Barrow than I thought," she said. "All of the same creatures are here."

Gingerly she took a small bite of the kelp blade—and

waited, recalling her father's words: "Take a little bite, and if it's not bitter it's edible." The kelp was drab and salty-tasting, but it was not bad. Emily ate a handful, then went back to the ship to look for something to carry it in. The salty weed made her thirsty, so she went back to her ice floe. She remembered having seen patches of old sea ice, called *piqaluyak*, [Pea-kal-lu-yak] on it. Her family drank melted *piqaluyak*. It was saltless—the most delicious water she ever tasted. She picked up the cooking kit's pot-like lid, climbed on the ice floe, and went right to the old ice. The dome shape of the ice told her that it was one or more years old, but it was fresh and drained of salt. Chipping out several pieces, she sucked on them until she was no longer thirsty. The rest she put in her cooking pot. It was too cold for it to melt. She ran back to her mattress camp.

"Thank you, Siku. You have led me to food and water." She laughed. "And *I* was supposed to save *you*."

Having eaten and drunk, she thought about how to get home. The modern life of the Eskimo had not taught her how to live off the land.

"And," she said, "there will be no Siku on the land to guide me . . . Or will there?"

21

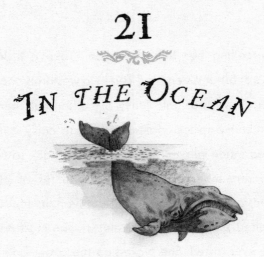

IN THE OCEAN

—— 1980 ——

Before *he left Smith Bay,* ⁓⁓⁓⁓ *had*
lingered as if caught in some shaman wizardry. He had seen the girl on the beach when he'd
held his head out of the water by pumping his flukes.
Now he rose again and looked. After many seconds,
he threw himself backward.

BOOM! He came up headfirst. The girl turned
around and smiled. He looked into her eyes. Something otherworldly passed between the eighty-ton
whale and the girl with the kind eyes, eyes like others
he had known. Siku recognized the same feeling he'd
had when they first saw each other, after she and her

brother had scrambled down the ice pack in Barrow. Later, she had saved him, and then he knew he must save her.

"Siku, you're with me," she called. "You have brought me here. I'll make it."

~~~~~~~ sank back into the water, and turning onto his belly, joined a group of whales. The girl turned her boots west and walked down the beach.

Emily Toozak and Siku were one spirit.

22

ON THE LAND

—— 1980 ——

Siku met three other whales and swallowed five hundred pounds of plankton. They were headed for deeper water. The sun was circling the earth just above the horizon. In its gold light Siku spy hopped as if to check on Emily Toozak, then dove and swam out of Smith Bay.

Emily Toozak was also ready to leave the bay. She gathered a few things from the ship that might be useful on her trip, including a wooden box, and put them in her blanket. Taking a deep breath, she swung the blanket on her back, tied the ends around her chest, and left the battered wreck.

She heard a thunderous *whoosh* . . . and turned around.

A whale spy hopped, dove, and slowly lifted its great head. The figure on its chin was a dancing Eskimo man, hands up, knees bent and far apart. She waved. "I'll see you, Siku. I am well," she called, and began to walk.

A familiar voice traveled clearly to Siku. Then he heard a chorus of shrieks, tings, and roars. The sounds were calling him, telling him the route to the next good feeding area.

Emily Toozak sighed as she watched Siku's footprints leave the bay.

Frightened, she sat back down. Then, like some spirit out of a shaman's brew, a gossamer wind of mist blew over her. Although she was alone, she no longer felt afraid.

Siku, that's you, she imagined. *I feel you. You are with me. I am all right now.* She lightly brushed her cheek with her hand.

She stood up and started on her journey.

"Siku," she said to the mist, "I will find berries on the tundra and ground squirrels in the grass. I am an Eskimo." She left the beach and stepped onto the seemingly endless tundra.

After a few steps, she gasped, wiped her eyes, and stared. "Is that somebody walking toward me?" The figure vanished in the sun.

"It's just a mirage," she sobbed. *"Ei eeee."* A misty wind blew softly against her face. Again, she touched her cheek, and became calm.

"Siku," she said. "You're with me. I will be all right," she repeated. It was a refrain she would say over and over.

23

IN THE OCEAN

— 1980 —

As 〜〜〜〜 *swam out of Smith Bay, he heard* distant *bzzt, bzzzt* sounds that he recognized to be narwhals! Narwhals are small whales, up to twenty feet long. The males have one long spear-like tooth growing out of their upper jaw resembling the mythical unicorn horn. Their flippers are shaped like half circles. Although narwhals live in the eastern Arctic waters of Greenland and Canada, a rare few had ventured as far west as Smith Bay. 〜〜〜〜 ignored them and followed the whale songs into the deeper Arctic water.

〜〜〜〜 swam past the coastal fringe of ice

floes as the sun warmed the polar region. When he surfaced for a breath, he glanced at the gulls and seals sitting on the floes. The water was growing warmer, the winds stronger, and there was ice to tumble in. Purple clouds sailed above green-and-yellow ones. Day and night were becoming one sun-filled day. He was near his summer home.

A storm threatened. A wolf eel darted in front him. A school of cod swirled and dove. The sun flashed gold on their scales. Jellyfish turned the water pink as the wind blew them together. The air temperature dropped to 30 degrees F. It snowed. ⌇⌇⌇⌇⌇ swam peacefully on. This was his world.

Miles farther along, the snow ended. A slick of zooplankton appeared near the ocean surface and ⌇⌇⌇⌇⌇ opened his gigantic mouth to take it in, but stopped. It smelled wrong. The slick was not the oil of rich zooplankton but a slick of oil from the motor-driven ships. Pumping his flukes up and down, he swam away from it.

When he reached the deeper waters, chatter told him that ⌇⌇⌇⌇⌇ was up ahead with three of his daughters and a son. The five had found each other by sound and sight despite the vastness of this sea. They ran their bodies along each other to express their whale pleasure at being together again. They pushed small ice floes back and forth and whipped their flukes in pleasure. ∼∿∿∿∿ joined them, carrying an ice chunk on his rostrum. ∿∿—–∿∿ knocked it off him and pushed it to his daughter.

The Eastern Beaufort Sea, the summer home of the bowhead whales, was murky with plankton and exploding with life. No other large baleen whales came here. These rich, ice-strewn waters were the waters of the ice whales.

Saffron cod summered here also. ∼∿∿∿∿ could see them eating zooplankton. Below them were castles of stone rising from the darkness like mysterious cities. On their sunlit walls, anemones and Arctic coral thrived. In the near darkness grew sponges and gelatinous creatures. Millions of years of evolution had adapted them and the bowhead whales to these impossible conditions. It was a world of variable light, cold water, and thick sea ice. There was nothing like these creatures anywhere else on the earth.

At home here, ∼∿∿∿∿ moved gently among the life on the edge of the ice pack.

Suddenly whale joy within ∼∿∿∿∿ stirred

him and he played with his friends and many of his own relatives. They breached and crashed into the water.

Playtime over, he checked his favorite zooplankton fields. There were pink masses of krill tumbling through the water column. Around the krill were animals that made sounds so vivid he could see them. He heard grunting fish, clicking shrimp, and whispering anemones.

After eating several tons of krill, he found his offspring again using sounds and listening. When they saw him they boomed whale words of happy recognition. *Whoosh.* CRASH! They slapped their flukes and touched their great bodies and ran their flukes across each other.

Then ∿∿∿∿∿ sought his larger family of cousins and second cousins and great-great-great-great-grandsons and daughters. They spy hopped joyfully, some of them rising forty feet above the surface of the water in bowhead exaltation.

The whales were coming back.

24

ON THE LAND

—— 1980 ——

Benny took Emily Toozak's mother Flossie's hand and held it firmly when he returned without her daughter.

"She is alive," he said. "And we will find her."

Robert and Oliver smiled hopelessly, their arms around Flossie's shoulders. Slowly they walked her home.

The shaman's curse? Could it be true? Robert thought. Glancing quickly from his son to his wife, he hoped they had not read his mind. He bent his head so they could not read his face.

Benny watched them walk toward their home. He stood on the black gravel beach stones alone. The ice, snow, wind, and clouds raced from horizon to horizon.

ON THE LAND

— 1980 —

Looking determinedly across the broad tundra, Emily Toozak searched for signs of a village, a snow machine, or a hunter. There were none. All was brown and green with splashes of blue or pink wildflowers. Ancient landscape left by the Ice Age on the tundra rippled toward the horizon. They were carpeted with moss and grass.

"No help there," she said aloud. "So I walk on. That's what I have legs for, Siku. You use your fins and flukes to get to the Beaufort Sea and back. I'll use my legs to get to Barrow."

Her grandmother had told her that her early ancestors would walk three hundred miles to visit their friends in the winter. When they reached their destination, they feasted, played games, and danced. Marriage matches were arranged between families. Then they all walked home.

"I can do that too, Siku. Go legs, go."

She returned to the beach for easier walking. Almost immediately she found patches of oyster leaf growing on the beach gravel where the waves had only lapped, not pounded. She snacked on their rubbery leaves. Large pinkish jellyfish stranded by the low tide and storms covered the beach. Their tentacles were a hundred feet long and looked like tangled hair.

The bells could be poisonous to eat, her grandfather had told her. She climbed the bluff back to the tundra. Now that Emily had to survive by herself, she found she remembered some of his lessons. Her grandfather had always talked about the old ways. She and Oliver had accompanied him on walks when they were small. Every day he had showed them a new plant to eat or creature to watch. As kids, they were usually more interested in playing tag rather than learning. Now Emily tried to recall the teachings of the Toozaks before her. She wished she had paid more attention then—she hoped her grandfather's lessons would come back to her now.

Walking on, she went around two-inch-high willow forests and vast gardens of dwarf buttercups. The Arctic crowberries were only in bud and not much good to her. By noon, and very hungry, she decided that buds must be good for one and ate handfuls of them. They were tasteless, but she ate them anyway. Hunger satisfied, she chanted as she walked.

> *"Siku, Siku, you are my spirit person.*
> *You have made the plants part of you and me.*
> *You have made the animals part of you and me.*
> *We flow through each other.*
> *We are one.*
> *Aye, ya, ya. Aye, ya, ya."*

Emily came upon a field of the first flowers to bloom, dwarf lupine. They were azure blue in color, like the shadows of sea ice. She knelt down to smell them. *Swish!*—a white-fronted goose flew up beside her.

And nearby in her nest lay eight unhatched eggs.

"Magic, Siku," she said, her dark eyes nearly closing with happiness. "Bird eggs are gold." She cracked two and eagerly drank their rich filling.

"For some bird species, if you take all of the eggs, Siku," she said, "they will lay again. But not geese, they will not lay more that season. So I better take just one or two from each nest." She paused. "Now, where did I learn that?" Was she remembering her grandfather's words on her own? Was Siku helping her?

Placing the blanket and egg box carefully on the ground, she stretched out to rest. As she started to close her eyes, she blinked them wide open. A bank of fog was moving toward her. She would need shelter, for Arctic fog was cold and blinding. She remembered the fog two years ago that swept down on the town so suddenly that she couldn't find her house and ended up huddling with some sled dogs.

Hurrying behind a frost heave, she opened her blanket and put the egg box and the little objects from the wreck on a patch of rubbery lichen. Quickly making a shelter out of the blanket by putting heavy stones on its edges, she crawled under it and waited for the fog to arrive.

It was then she heard the airplane. She burst out of the shelter.

"Oh, no!" she cried as the pilot saw the fogbank and turned away. The Wayne plane headed back to Barrow. Its motor sounded fainter and fainter.

"No! Don't go!" she called into the white, thick air.

The world went white as the fog enveloped her. She crawled back under her blanket and pulled her parka tighter to her body and blew into her hood to keep warm. Tears fell, but she quickly wiped them away.

"I've got eggs to eat and drinking ice in my pot. I'll be all right, Siku."

She stopped talking to listen to sheets of mist sweeping the tundra. A strong wind tore at her blanket. She held on to it.

The tundra was bursting with life after the fog lifted. There were lines of birds in the sky and small mammals scurrying on the tundra—all her friends. She had big goose eggs and little berry buds. Although she still had her fresh drinking ice, now that there were many freshwater ponds to drink from. She felt connected to the earth.

After the sun had circled the sky several more times, she came upon a pond that flowed into a river. She did not know the river's name, but since Siku had passed many river mouths without knowing their name, so would she.

The problem now was how to cross it. As Emily grew more comfortable with her surroundings, she began to think more clearly. Barrow lay somewhere on the other side of this river. The currents ran east north of Point Barrow, she figured. "I'm sure Siku pushed me until there was a safe place to beach. I must go west." So she walked up the river-bank looking for a shallow place to wade. She came upon a kayak partially buried in mud near a group of tall tussocks. The kayak was old but still usable. She pulled it out and rinsed it off.

"Siku," she called. "You sent this kayak here. I know you did." Smiling and laughing in play talk, she put it on the water. A paddle was left in the bow. She hopped in, loaded her gear, and paddled into the small river.

As she continued up the river, the wind stopped. Suddenly she was in a storm of mosquitoes. She had met them before and knew what to do—pull her parka hood tighter, then grin and bear it. Hundreds crept up her nose and swarmed on her lips. She ate them. They were good! Licking mosquitoes off her lips, savoring their sweet lemony taste, she headed west up the river.

Flies joined the mosquitoes until the air became gray. Both insects were biters. As Emily was wondering what she could do about that, a wind picked up that blew the insects away.

"Siku," she said, and patted her cheek.

She looked over and saw several big fat woolly-bear caterpillars on the riverbank.

"Oh, Siku," she said. "I know what to do. Arctic woolly bears freeze for the winter and can't move. Ernest said it takes them fourteen years of freezing and thawing before they can become a moth. They have thawed now. I'll try eating them."

The flies began biting again as she ate a woolly bear. She scooped up a handful of snow from a last patch on the north side of the riverbank. She held it near her face. Cold emanated from it. The flies flew away.

As she was paddling she felt something with her feet in the bow of the kayak. She pulled it out; it was a small gillnet.

"*Aarigaa* (great)! Now I can get all the food I need!"

She set the net in an eddy in the river, and within minutes, it was filled with whitefish. She pulled out the net with its savory catch and cleaned the silvery fish with the same knife she had used to cut Siku's ropes. She patted her cheek. She was hungry, and after slicing the fish into small pieces, she ate the sweet meat. A feeling of well-being came over her. She packed the other fish away for later.

Emily Toozak kept paddling. After four more miles she came to a lake that connected to another creek, and another lake, and on and on. She kept heading west. She thought of the long journey her whale made each year. The thought of Siku surviving all those years of Yankee whaling made her believe she could survive too.

She saw a patch of yellow flowers on the bank. They were like nothing else she had ever seen. They were little cups instead of petals, the northern water carpet. She peered into the cups. Shiny seeds lay heaped in the center of each. A drop of water fell from her fingertips into a cup. The seeds splashed out in all directions.

"A splash cup," she said, and laughed. "What a smart way to sow your seeds. Plants have wondrous ways. If plants can be that clever, so can I."

Tired of paddling, she pulled up to the bank. She tore from her blanket three quarter-inch-wide strips and braided them into a rope. Then she tied a couple of shorter braided ropes to it. At the ends of each, she tied stones.

"I've made a bola, Siku," she said proudly, and whirled it around her head. "The snare of my ancestors." She let it go and watched it career through the air.

"Pretty good." She ran to it and picked it up. Walking as quietly as a ptarmigan, she looked for game. Not far away was an Arctic fox that had almost finished changing into his brown summer coat. He was catching lemmings. She circled the bola over her head and hurled it. The fox darted away. She felt discouraged. The fox was too fast and wary.

Then she remembered that bolas are meant for hunting birds. She was suddenly remembering things other elders in the village beside her grandfather had said all the while she was growing up. She thought she had not paid attention.

She walked on, throwing the bola at ptarmigan and owls. She got better. She whirled it into a flock of geese and, surprisingly, struck one. She grabbed it and hurriedly plucked and cleaned it. She had real food.

"But I have no fire," she moaned, and then happened to glance at her wristwatch; its glass covering magnified the numerals. Magnifying glasses could make fire. That she had learned in school. She worked the glass off the watch, crumpled the cotton band, gathered dry grass, and broke up the wooden box wrapping her one remaining goose egg in her blanket.

Then she dug a pit in the thawed surface ground and lined it with stones. Getting down on her knees, she concentrated the rays of the sun on the grass bundle. The dry blades grew red and burst into flame. She fed the flame with pieces of the wooden box and slivers of driftwood. When the fire was burning hot, she added stones and let them heat. When they were fiery red, she wrapped the goose in grass and then got the fish from her kayak. She cleaned and wrapped them, too. She placed it all in the pit on top of the hot stones, and covered it with damp grass.

"I am a part of everything—the grass, the tundra, birds in the sky, especially my ice whale in the sea."

Emily Toozak sang a song and gathered green edible plants while the goose cooked. When she thought the stones were cool, she uncovered the food. She tore off a goose leg and bit into it. It was delicious. She feasted on goose and fish until she was full. With it she ate some scurvy grass leaves and drank from the fresh cool water from the creek.

"I'm doing good, Siku," she said as a misty wind caressed her face. She touched her cheek again.

The sun was in the sky day and night, so Emily Toozak slept when the animals slept—noon and midnight. As she lay down to sleep one noon, she thought about the workday the white men had brought to the Arctic. It was a strict hourly schedule from 9:00 A.M. to 5:00 P.M. in spite of the Arctic's two-month-long day and two-month-long night each year.

Out here, she was following the rhythm of her world.

Emily Toozak was refreshed when she awoke. She got quickly to her feet, packed her goose, fish, and treasures, and got back in the kayak. She paddled around ponds, creeks, past fox dens, scared the ground squirrels along the banks, and listened to Arctic loons call. She felt a part of them all.

She needed to make sure that she was heading west, so she watched the sun and remembered the wind almost always blew from the east. The sun and wind were her compass.

Finally the creek opened up into another bay. Walking up the beach, she came upon the gigantic bones of a bowhead whale that had washed up long ago. She ran to them. Whale bones were everywhere, old ones like the ones from which her people sculpted art and made tools. She wandered among them, stepping over huge jawbones and plunking herself down on vertebrae as big as tussocks. The whale ribs, she realized, could make frames for shelters.

"Siku," she said, "what big bones you have!" She laughed, ate more of her goose, drank some water, and napped. It was a sunny, calm midnight.

When she nodded awake, she was aware that the winds had changed. Clouds were blowing in from the Chukchi Sea.

That could mean trouble, she worried.

Hurriedly she rolled several large vertebrae high on the beach close to the tundra grasses and placed them in a circle. She covered them with the big broad whale shoulder blades to make a roof. All the bones were heavy, but she worked hard.

Emily Toozak was still working on her whale-bone house when the first snowflakes arrived. She dug a hollow in the pebbles inside and lined it with the remains of her blanket.

Making sure her house was strong, she went outside and pushed against it with the force she supposed the wind might have. She had hardly tested it when loping out of the waves came a seal pup. He walked up to her on flippers and stomach crying real tears. She picked him up and held him close.

"Natchiayaaq," she said, "where is your mother? A storm is coming."

The baby seal looked at her. Hugging him close, she crawled back into her house and sat down with him in her arms. When he stopped wiggling, she fed him some goose breast. He gobbled it up.

"My hot-water bottle," she said when she realized how warm the seal was. "I am going to need you." She tucked him into her parka.

The wind struck. The massive bones held.

For three days the storm raged. Food and water ran out at the end of the third day. The pup became restless. He cried in a mother-calling voice.

"Maybe he knows his mother is near, Siku," she said. "I feel you want me to set him free."

The door, however, was crusted with ice and snow. She kicked it hard to clear it off. When it fell open, there was the sun, white gold and beautiful. Reluctantly she put her "hot-water bottle" on the pebbles. Natchiayaaq was free. He loped off toward the water.

"Natchiayaaq, don't leave yet." But he was gone.

Two heads swam off through the waves, a big one and a little one. She smiled.

Emily Toozak gathered her things, tied on her pack and walked to the tundra.

26

ON THE LAND

—— 1980 ——

Along the beach ran a bluff. Emily Toozak climbed it to have a look around and saw a caribou standing apart from a small herd nearby. She ducked down; she was afraid the caribou would run when he saw her.

She dropped to her knees and crept toward him. When she was nearer she could see that he was limping. His head was low. He couldn't run. Should she wait until he stumbled and fell? No, she didn't have the time to wait. She crept on toward him wondering how she would kill such a big animal with just her knife.

A melodic song arose. She looked up. Five wolves

pranced on their long legs along the rim of the horizon. She stopped moving. She would watch. To run might be an invitation to the wolves to chase her. The wind was blowing her scent away from them and she was safe for the moment.

Suddenly she wanted to sneeze. But she pinched her nose and "achooed" into the moss. Peeking through the hairs of the fur on her parka, she saw that in that instant the wolves had attacked the caribou and their snarlings had covered her sneeze.

They were intent only on finding food and quickly put the caribou out of his misery and pain.

With their great jaws they splintered the bones, tore into the hide, and ate his liver for the vitamins they would get. Then they ate meat. When they were full, they went back over the horizon, presumably to their whelping den and the pups inside it.

Emily Toozak jumped to her feet and ran to the carcass. She cut off large pieces of meat, picked up her gear, and started to run. She wanted to leave the wolves' caribou far behind before she stopped. No one had told her how gentle wolves could be.

Back at camp by the bay, she sat down to dig an oven and build a fire to cook the delicious meat. Driftwood was scattered all along the beach. There was more than enough to make a nice fire.

"Siku, thank you. You are really protecting me."

She looked about. The land was still endless. Birds called, a wolf howled. But something had changed. A weight had been lifted off her shoulders.

She wheeled around and faced the bay.

"Siku," she called. She was quiet for several minutes. There was no answer. Siku was far away, but his spirit was here, with her.

Then she stood up and faced the sea, her arms reaching out.

"Siku, Siku,
The shaman's curse is gone.
Gone, gone, aye, aye, aye.
The shaman's curse is in the wind.
Aye, aye, aye."

Three weeks had passed since she had been pulled overboard. When the meat was cooked, she ate it. Then she slept. Then she got up and walked up the coast to the north.

27

ON THE OCEAN

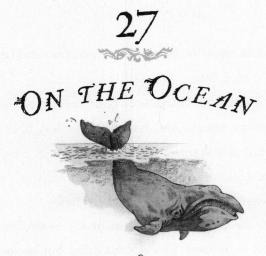

——— 1980 ———

The ship North Star *motored north through the* Bering Strait and into the Arctic Ocean. It was June and Captain Tom "Tommy" Boyd V was standing on the deck fighting the wind.

"What a beautiful sight," he said to Will, his twenty-two-year-old son and now the ship's first mate. He laughed. "Our ancestors would never have said that about the Arctic. It was frightening to them. Imagine bringing a sailing ship past those islands in the Bering Strait and then into this ice-covered ocean in 1848!"

Will nodded and watched the Arctic birds through

his binoculars. With his keen interest in birds, he was fascinated by all the new species he was seeing—murres, guillemots, shearwaters, eiders, and auklets—to name a few.

"I hope the bowheads will increase in numbers," Captain Boyd said. "No whalers except certain Eskimo communities can take them now." The president of the United States had even recently signed the Endangered Species Act, and the whales were now included on that list.

Captain Boyd strode back to the chart house and took the wheel. He steered the ship up the west coast of Alaska to deliver its cargo of merchandise the Eskimos had ordered from catalogs a year ago.

Near Wainwright, the ice was almost gone, and with it the seals and walrus. Fulmars, stout birds with a four-foot wingspan, were hunting fish as they circled above the Chukchi Sea. The young of the brant geese, yellow-billed loons, and eider ducks flew among them, strengthening their wings for their August migration. Sandpipers tiptoed in lines down to and back from the water as they hunted food. Will was enthralled. He had wanted to see these birds since his dad had taken the helm of the *North Star* six years ago and brought back stories about the wildlife in the north. Will knew then what he wanted to do—study birds in the Arctic.

Captain Boyd anchored the ship at the coastal town of Olgoonik [ul-GOO-nik], now called Wainwright, to unload some cargo. When the goods that the Eskimos had ordered had been carried ashore, the captain piloted the ship on to Barrow.

At Barrow, he anchored the *North Star* some distance offshore in deep water, as the town has no harbor. With the ship secure, he leaned on the rail and watched the men unload the freight into launches which could come ashore on Barrow's beach.

Will joined him and leaned on the rail beside his dad, looking at all the boxes of freight. Gas stoves, table lamps, and more would be unloaded at Barrow. Everyone assumed that Eskimos still lived according to the old ways, but he knew that they had many modern conveniences just like everyone else.

Although Will's ancestors had been Yankee whalers, the Boyds had turned to merchant shipping once the whaling industry disappeared. They kept returning to the Arctic Ocean. It was in their blood. But Will was more interested in zoology than in boats. He was coming north as an ornithologist, not as a merchant shipper. He had graduated from Cornell University with a degree in ornithology. He loved to be with his father when he navigated these waters.

He glanced at the thermometer on the deck. It read 30 degrees F. It was the end of August.

"Freezing in the dog days," he said, and laughed.

"Just a late summer's day up here," Captain Tommy replied, and turned to a sailor. "Order a launch to go ashore. I'm going to town to eat at the Mexican restaurant at the Top of the World Hotel." He grinned. "Best burritos in the whole country."

Over the VHF radio, they heard a whaling crew calling back to town, reporting the successful harvest of a young bowhead miles away. It would take several hours for all the boats to tow it back to the beach. There it would be shared among the thankful and hardworking community. The crew gathered round as they listened to the details of the report.

"Let's go watch them pull it up on the beach," Will said.

The launch arrived and they went ashore.

28

ON THE LAND

—— 1980 ——

Will and his dad walked to the north edge of the village and joined the villagers to help pull the forty-ton whale up on land. They stayed to watch it being butchered. The meat, *maktak* [muk-tuk] (skin with blubber), and baleen were put on sleds. The villagers took their prize home joyfully. Nothing was better to eat than bowhead whale. When all of it had been distributed and the women had cut off the last bit of meat from the bones, Will took out his binoculars and focused on the birds again. Suddenly an Arctic gyrfalcon streaked before him, pursuing a ptarmigan.

"I think I'll stay ashore awhile, Dad, and look around," he called to his father, who was heading for the restaurant.

"Okay. Radio for a launch when you're ready."

Thrilled to be finding birds he had never seen before, he started walking. He walked until a car stopped and offered him a ride to the trading post. Suddenly, he realized he was cold. He jumped in and rode to the post and went inside for a cup of coffee. Before long, he was conversing with the man who worked on an exploratory oil rig in a remote area. Fascinated by of the complexity of the project, Will began to ask a lot of questions.

"Hey, I'm flying out there for a few hours," the man said. "I have a small Cessna airplane. Want to come with me?" Will immediately accepted and radioed his father to tell him. The pilot loaned him a warm parka and polar boots. They flew to Cape Simpson.

As he stepped out of the plane on the remote airstrip, he saw a rare Mongolian plover fly by.

"Wow, I'm going to follow that bird, if you don't mind," he said to the pilot. "It's a new one for me."

"Okay, but keep the rig in sight. I'll meet you back here in two hours."

Will knew that the Mongolian plover was very rare in this area and so he followed it. Soon he found himself far out on the tundra.

And then, suddenly, the fog set in and he was lost.

Whiteouts are one of the perils of the Arctic. He tried to orient himself by the sun, but it was no help. The fog was too dense and the sun never set in the Arctic to tell him which way was west. His dad had once said that in the far Arctic the sun sets first to the north. So in which direction was the oil rig? Were the birds flying *to* it or *away* from it?

He looked north. Nothing. He turned a complete circle, and there on the horizon for a brief instant, were the distant poles and cranes of the rig. Then the fog quickly set in again. He tried to maintain a heading toward the rig, walking for hours. When the fog lifted again, there was no rig in sight. He had walked the wrong way and was lost.

An Eskimo appeared in the distance, coming toward him. Will sighed with relief. The man could lead him back to the airstrip where the Cessna had landed. He waited.

The Eskimo turned into a young woman carrying a sack on her back. When he saw her, he burst into a jog.

"Help me," Will said. "I'm lost."

"I am too!" said Emily.

They stared at each other, smiled, and burst into laughter. Her face was brown with sunshine, her smile framed beautiful teeth, and her dark eyes sparkled.

"Oh, look, could that be the oil rig?" she asked pointing to a faint object on the skyline. Will turned around.

"Yes," he said, "it is," and began to walk toward it. He faltered and stopped.

"Wait, I think that's a mirage. We should be going this way," he said, and started walking in the wrong direction again.

She grabbed him by the shoulder, turned him around, and faced him toward the distant rig.

"Walk," said Emily Toozak. She took his hand and pulled. "I'm Emily Toozak."

Will's feet felt cold and tired. But he went toward the rig step by reluctant step. While they walked Emily Toozak told him an amazing tale of living on the tundra for three weeks, with a whale for a guide, and as he listened to her words, Will forgot he was lost. He had no idea that Emily had been missing for almost a month. She seemed so oddly comfortable with her situation. The rig grew larger and more distinct with each step they took toward it.

"You say a bowhead whale saved you?" he asked as they came to the runway and walked onto it. She looked him straight in his eyes.

"Yes," she said, "but now I'm back in civilization. I have to radio my parents and let them know I'm safe." She smiled a million words.

He believed her story. The Arctic was unlike any place

he'd been before. He felt like anything could happen here.

The pilot had been patiently waiting for his passenger for hours. He was worried the young man had gotten lost in the fog. He knew how unforgiving this country could be. He, Emily, and Will ducked and climbed into the small Cessna and took off to the west.

The airplane rolled to a stop on the Barrow tarmac and Will climbed out. He reached up to give Emily Toozak a hand, but she was still sitting, her eyes closed. He thought he heard her whispering, "Siku."

Emily Toozak opened her eyes, pulled her hood over her head, and climbed out of the plane. She walked slowly across the tarmac to the passenger terminal, up the steps, and into the building. She gave a whoop and ran forward. There were her parents, Benny, his son James, and Oliver. The pilot had radioed ahead that she had been found and was in good health, and the airport had called her parents. It was a small town.

At home, she was greeted by her family and dozens of friends. She was overwhelmed to be back with so many people she loved. The village seemed huge. Her mother had roasted a caribou shank and brought out the best of the summer's berries. Emily thought of the last caribou and plants she had eaten. When they were done, Emily Toozak spoke quietly of her adventures.

Robert Toozak took her hand when she was finished.

"Emily Toozak," he said, "do you really think that Siku pushed your floe to shore and saved your life?"

"Yes, I do. The curse is lifted," she replied, though she believed in her heart it was never a curse. "We both have helped each other."

Later, Benny beat his dance drum far into the night.

Not many days after this, Will applied for and got a job at the Navy Research Lab.

In a few years, he and Emily Toozak were married.

They named their firstborn son Agvik (meaning "whale"), with no numerals. The Toozak curse had been lifted. That was the year 1989.

29

ON THE LAND

───── 2005 ─────

Looking out the doorway of the Alaska Airlines jet plane, TJ, Captain Tommy Boyd's second grandson, stared out at Barrow. No trees graced the landscape. Telephone poles and small gray wooden buildings dominated the land. An occasional yellow or blue house speckled the village like flowers. In the distance, a bowhead whale jaw loomed in front of the town hall, dwarfing the people walking by it. Here and there, snow still lingered.

The view the other way was quite different. Snow and an occasional patch of tundra grass stretched on a flat and endless landscape to the horizon.

"Move quickly," said a well-meaning passenger on the steps that led down to the tarmac. "It's cold!"

TJ raced down the steps onto the runway. Gusts of wind nearly blew him off his feet. Flying snow stung him. He ducked his head into his parka hood. Struggling to keep his balance, he reached the steel steps of the terminal building and climbed them. The open steel mesh of the steps let the ice and snow fall to the ground underneath. No one had to shovel. TJ liked that.

"And this is the month of May!?" he shouted into the wind.

Inside, he found himself in a modern terminal. Passengers were wearing furs and heavy boots. This was just another day in the Arctic.

A boy walked up to him.

"Hi," he said. "You must be TJ Boyd from Massachusetts. He extended his hand. "I am Agvik Boyd, your cousin."

TJ blinked and stared. He was really here in Barrow. He had heard about the Arctic from the part of his family and especially Agvik, his cousin, who lived here. Now he was meeting one of them for the first time. He was almost speechless.

"Let's get your baggage," Agvik said. "The lab truck is

waiting outside. You must be tired after traveling for so long."

"Let's go." TJ grabbed one big duffel bag, Agvik the other.

Their boots squeaked in the cold as they crunched down the front steps to the truck. Agvik gestured to TJ to get in the truck and climbed into the driver's seat beside him.

The truck was heated, but TJ was still cold by the time they reached the lab beside the still-frozen ocean. It was May 2. The temperature was 12 degrees F. They stomped the snow off their feet and entered the building.

Agvik said, "You're going to bunk with me here at the research lab. We're with the college guys. They're counting bowhead whales."

"That's what we're here for, right?" TJ asked. Agvik's dad was an ornithologist, but he worked with scientists who studied whales and recorded whale songs.

"Yeah, but for now you and I are on our own. Come with me."

TJ picked up his duffel and followed Agvik down a dark corridor to a room lined with bunks.

"Pick one not being used," Agvik said, waving his hand at the beds stacked closely together in the room.

TJ threw his duffel on an empty bunk and took off his parka.

"Let's eat," said Agvik, and led TJ down the hall to a large kitchen with a stove, a refrigerator, a long table, chairs, and all kinds of groceries.

"Every man for himself," Agvik said, and smiled. His black eyes sparkled under ragged bangs. TJ noticed that his face was narrower than the other Eskimos'. It looked like a Boyd face. Agvik's dad and TJ's dad were brothers.

A VHF radio crackled nearby.

"Ice camp calling," Agvik said of the noise. "That's where they're counting the whales." TJ looked curious.

Agvik responded to TJ's expression. "The camp's on the ice near shore, where it's grounded to the ocean floor. It's only four feet thick this year, but perfectly safe." He smiled. Eskimos as well as other scientists from the Lower Forty-eight had come to count the whales. They wanted to know if their populations were increasing, decreasing, or staying the same.

"What do you want to do now?" Agvik asked.

All of the sudden exhaustion came over TJ. He'd been traveling for nearly twenty-four hours. "Go to bed," he said. "It's nearly midnight!"

"Okay, first lesson," Agvik said, and smiled, "Pull this ski hat over your eyes and pretend it's dark." He tossed it to him. TJ fell into his bed fully clothed.

When he woke up, Agvik was not around. He wished he were. But his stomach told him what to do. He went to the kitchen and fixed himself a bowl of cereal. He ate it on a big wooden table cluttered with tools, data sheets, electronic parts, pencils, and equipment.

"You're up," called Agvik as he entered the room. "Want to go out to ice camp, TJ?"

"Oh, boy, do I." He was excited to finally be able to see the Arctic!

They pulled old air-force insulated jumpsuits over their clothes and walked out into the wind. A snow machine with a sled attached was waiting for them. TJ was told to ride on the rear of the sled. Hesitatingly he stepped up on it and grabbed the back handle of the sled. Two scientists sat in warm furs on another sled with some valuable equipment packed in coolers—not to keep it cool but to keep it from freezing.

With a lurch they were off. They sped around Quonset huts, crossed a road, and bumped out onto the land-fast sea ice. Then they crossed onto the frozen Arctic Ocean.

Seeing it, TJ was glad that Agvik had mentioned that the ice was four feet thick and safe.

TJ stared at the white wilderness around him as they thumped around blue blocks of ice. Next they roared down a winding ice trail, bounced over ridges, and rode smoothly on frozen lakes of flat sea ice. Six miles later, they arrived at three tents and a small wooden lab shed sitting on its own sled. The tents had been set up behind a pressure ridge.

TJ gladly disembarked. There was an Eskimo whaling camp on the other side of the pressure ridge on a shelf of ice. TJ stared at the huge ridge.

A light wind was blowing across the ice. Suddenly, almost before he could walk around the tents, the light wind became a westerly gale.

"Break camp," shouted an Eskimo over the radio. All of a sudden everyone was in motion. Students collapsed the tents and tossed gear on the sleds behind the snowmobiles. One student attached the lab sled to his snowmobile and drove off.

With a muffled boom, the thicker pack ice hit the thinner land-fast ice and began piling and shattering the ice, creating another pressure ridge.

One of the scientists grabbed TJ's parka and pulled him

up beside him on the back of his sled. They jerked forward. A crack opened up where TJ had stood, widened, and carried the empty science camp to sea.

"You have to do what the Eskimos do out here," said the scientist as they careened toward the new campsite. "The Eskimos who were camped at the very edge of the ice left minutes before we arrived. They knew the danger in that wind. I sure didn't. We also need to learn to break camp as fast as they do. They can do it in five minutes."

"It was so nice and calm before it hit," TJ said.

An hour later, they found a new campsite. Students started pitching tents.

TJ grabbed a tent off their sled and pitched it. It was a sleeping tent for four people. TJ saw what needed to be done and carried the huge sleeping bags inside the tent.

The students, who had left before TJ, already had the food tent set up and were studying this ice to determine where to put the lab sled. TJ figured it must be near open water so the hydrophones could pick up and record the bleeps, blips, shrieks, growls, and moans of the bowheads talking. It also had to be far enough away to be safe from the dangerous, shifting sea ice. Camping on the ice was a complex and risky business.

Fifteen minutes later, the radio crackled as a student scientist said the underwater listening instruments were in the sea, and ice camp was in business again.

"That was a close call," said Ray, a student from Ohio. "We should have known better than to think we knew as much as the Eskimo whalers about the dangers of the ice." He thought a minute. "They see more whales than we do too—and without binoculars."

"How do they do that?" TJ asked.

"A thousand years of experience," said Ray. "And they pass on this knowledge from generation to generation through stories."

"Members of my family were whalers long ago," said TJ. "Guess this is the new way to watch whales—with your ears."

That night TJ and his cousin returned to the research lab from a long day at whale camp. TJ wearily pulled a ski hat over his eyes and went to sleep.

30

IN THE OCEAN

——— 2005 ———

"‿᙭᙭᙭‿᙭᙭᙭ !!!!!!!!!!!!" shrilled ‿\\\᙭᙭\\\᙭ He sent out a danger-enemy warning to all the whales within hearing distance.

Several younger whales heard the warning, thinking it meant killer whales were near. Confused, they swam toward the elder whale.

This was not what ‿\\\᙭᙭\\\᙭ had meant to warn them about. He had no "words" for what was happening. This threat came from dark bullet-shaped ships.

KABOOOOM! KABOOOOM!

The ships were towing seismic air guns. With these

instruments they were sounding the deep ocean bottom for oil. The sounds hurt the whales' ears and impaired their direction-finding senses.

〜〜〜〜〜, who was also in the area, spy hopped so he could see the ships. When he fell back, the sounds stung and burned him. He could not hear the familiar songs of the Arctic Ocean—crabs clicking, fish popping, seals warbling. He became confused. Some years back a young female trying to reach the coastal currents swam into a giant ship's propellers and was killed. Large ships were dangerous.

〜〜〜〜〜 realized that the noises were confusing him too. He was going the wrong way. He turned around. There before him was a seismic gunship. He had tolerated the icebreakers that came every winter. He could adjust to airplanes. But the sounds of the seismic air guns were painful.

His group joined him and swam steadily until they were far beyond the seismic air-gun ships that were sounding for oil. Then 〜〜〜〜〜 heard the voice of 〜〜〜〜〜. The old whale was swimming toward him. He was acting strangely. He lolled from side to side, stopped, and then sped up. The seismic sounds had injured his tender ears. He could not balance himself well enough to swim. He growled in distress.

~~~~~ took a position before him and led him to the shallower shore currents. The two elders joined the other whales now streaming past Barrow, going east.

~~~~~ felt a warm river in the current. The thread of warmth was streaming out of the Pacific Ocean through the Bering Strait. He had never felt water from the Pacific that was this warm in the 150 years of his lifetime. His ocean was changing.

31

ON THE OCEAN

——— 2005 ———

"**P**ull this white parka over the one you have on," Agvik said to TJ. "It makes it harder for the whales to see you." He tossed the garment to TJ and donned another. "They're wind- and waterproof. We might get splashed.

"I'm hoping that Siku will be coming back. He comes here about this time every year."

"You mean you've seen him, the same whale our ancestor saw being born?" TJ asked.

"Same one! Siku's one big whale, probably weighs a hundred tons, and changes the sea level when he breaches!" Agvik laughed. "And today I hope you'll see him too." They were going to paddle out a ways in a kayak to search for the whale.

After the seismic ships had gone, a group of whales took the northeastward-flowing current at Point Barrow and swam close to the last of the land-fast ice. Moving like an armada, these magnificent swimmers occasionally rose out of the water to breathe and spy on the land-fast ice. To ～～/ＭＭＷＭ this day, the ice was too silent . . . no birds, no barking seals, just stillness. Then he heard hunters whispering.

"～～～～～～～～～～～～～～～～～～～～～～～～～～～～～

～～～～～～～～～～～～～～～～～～～～～～～～～～～ ."

Siku warned the other whales away. But he didn't swim with them. There was something about these hunters that made him stay.

～／ＭＭＷＭ looked through the water but could not see them. He swam closer to the land-fast ice and was able to make out their shadows. They were blue, in the light cast by the orange midnight sun.

～／ＭＭＷＭ dove deep. The other whales had turned abruptly when Siku warned them. Instead of joining them, he swam to a large ice floe not far from shore. It had been a long time since he had seen a descendant of the people with the kind eyes. There was another boy with him. They were above him. ~᳘ᔈᔈᔈ᳘ swam under the ice shelf and pushed up a breathing crack.

He took a breath, swam out from under it, and surfaced not far from the boys. They gasped as he breached forty feet in the air. The Eskimo dancing figure shone out, and the fallback wave rose ten feet high and raced toward them.

"Siku!" Agvik gasped.

Agvik's voice sent a ringed seal lumbering off the edge of an ice floe into the crest of ~᳘ᔈᔈᔈ᳘'s wave. She swam through a swarm of Arctic cod that ~᳘ᔈᔈᔈ᳘ had stirred up with his thundering tidal wave of a splash. She did not try to grab one but streamed on.

Agvik, unlike the seal, found the wave from this wild world a physical challenge. He turned the kayak, with TJ in the back, headfirst into it and rode it out without upsetting the craft.

"Close," said TJ.

"Paddle," Agvik hollered. "Siku is here."

They skimmed over the sea like king eiders and paddled toward Siku's footprints.

Not far from them ᔈᔈᔈ, who was now

very old, came swimming by. The seismic distur-
bances still irritated him. He turned from his group
and swam toward the boys. Their blue shadows
on the water told him where they were. When
he was close to them, he breached, thrust his
hundred-ton body backward, and sent an Arctic tidal
wave over the kayak. Bubbling and frothing, the
water rushed back to the sea.

~~~∿∿∿~~ felt the rage of his old mentor, swam
under the ice shelf to his breathing crack, and hung still.

⫽⫽∿∿⫼⫼ did not follow ~~∿∿~∿∿~ . . . . The
sea ice had roiled and banged against him, irritat-
ing the old whale more. He breached and lunged at
Agvik and TJ in their boat. He thrashed, an angry
animal that sailors call a "rogue whale."

"What's going on?" TJ asked. "Is that Siku again?"

"No," said Agvik. "It's another old male, not Siku."
He felt a fear he had not felt when Siku was present.

Agvik and TJ paddled fiercely to get away from
the whale. ⫽⫽∿∿⫼⫼ twisted, changed his direction,
and came at them in a wave of motion.

"Hold your breath, TJ," Agvik shouted.

TJ took a deep breath. The kayak turned upside

down. Agvik righted the craft with a stroke of his paddle. When they surfaced in the numbing water, TJ was spluttering and Agvik was wet but calm. Although chilled, they were warm enough in their Eskimo clothing.

Alarmed, Siku swam toward the old whale. He edged up to him and, using his whole body, pushed ⌐⑈⌒⌒⌒⑉⌐ away from the boys. ⌐⑈⌒⌒⌒⑉⌐ slapped his tail in frustration. And then he was gone.

Siku surfaced. His eye met Agvik's kind eyes—two lives that were laced together.

Safe on the ice, their coats shedding water, Agvik and TJ stared at each other. They pulled the kayak onto the ice then.

"Siku!" TJ yelled, and pointed to a whale that has risen from the water. "I saw him! He had a mark like an Eskimo dancer on his chin." An ivory gull flew under the azure sky.

"Let's go home," Agvik said, and turned around. Before them, a fog was blowing in. It quickly erased sea and sky.

"What do we do now?" TJ yelled through the fog.

"Sit still," Agvik answered.

The fog grew thicker. TJ could not even see their nearby kayak. He didn't know up from down. He felt dizzy.

"I'm dizzy," he gasped to Agvik.

"Close your eyes. It will pass."

TJ closed his eyes.

"Here's some *maktak* [muk-tuk]," Agvik said. "Whale blubber. Eat it and you will feel better." TJ waved his hand blindly until he felt Toozak's hand and the *maktak*.

"It's sliced thin, just eat it," he said.

TJ ate the light, nutty-tasting skin and fat and forgot his predicament. He felt new strength and a deep warmth return to his body. The more he ate, the better it tasted, and the better it tasted, the more he forgot the fog. Hours passed.

After what seemed like a long, long time, TJ spoke.

"I'm cold," he said. "My teeth are chattering."

"Swing your arms and eat more *maktak*," Agvik instructed.

The fog began to thin and there in the haze before them was a ghost-like figure.

"Who's that?" came a voice out of the whiteness.

"Agvik and TJ Boyd," Agvik answered.

A tall man emerged as the fog thinned.

"I'm Dr. Diaz," he said. "What are you doing out here?"

"I could ask you the same question!" responded Agvik. "We were trying to find a whale."

TJ stomped his feet and beat his arms to get warm.

"I'm with the lab," Dr. Diaz explained. "I was sampling seawater for an acidity test. We want to find out how the acidity of the water is changing due to the increase of carbon dioxide in the air." The boys could see him more clearly as the fog lifted and swept away.

Whoosh! A whale blew nearby.

Agvik turned around.

"Siku!" he yelled when he saw the whale's chin.

"You seem to know that whale," Dr. Diaz said.

"I do," Agvik answered. "He has been part of our family for many generations."

"That's valuable information. We are just finding out that whales are the oldest mammals on earth. The chemical composition of the eye suggests that some are two hundred years old. But we don't know for sure."

"There have been old stone harpoon points found in some whales' bodies," Agvik said. "They have been out of use for over one hundred and twenty-five years,"

"Really?" said TJ.

"Yeah, the last time they used that type of stone harpoon was back in the 1800s. So the whale in which they found it must have been older than that. He could have been big and old when he was struck and got away. Siku will be a hundred and fifty-seven in July," commented Agvik.

"You know that?" asked Dr. Diaz.

"Yes, I know when Siku was born," he said proudly.

"That's unusual. When?"

"Eighteen forty-eight. My ancestor saw his birth. It's a long story. My family has been protecting him ever since. We call him Siku. And he even saved my mother, and might have saved us today."

"Very interesting."

"My ancestors have passed this information to each generation in stories," Agvik said. "Seeing Siku now confirms his age."

"Hmm. But how do you recognize him?"

"He has a mark like a dancing Eskimo on his chin. It's a man—arm up, feet apart, and knees bent."

"A recognizable mark?" asked Dr. Diaz.

"Yes, that was Siku. He comes about this time every year."

Dr. Diaz looked at TJ, who was still shivering.

"Let's go to my tent and get warm," he said. "We'll have some food. This information you have is like finding the five-million-year-old prehuman Ardi skull. Amazing!" He smiled.

Agvik knew his whale was important. He felt good.

The fog lifted and there was Dr. Diaz's tent, only a short walk away. They went inside, where a Coleman stove burned. TJ, still damp from the kayak, wasted no time warming his hands and backside. The first thing Dr. Diaz did was to radio to headquarters. He told the dispatcher to tell Agvik's family that he and TJ were safe and with him. Then he made coffee and peanut butter sandwiches while talking enthusiastically about Siku.

"Since he has such a distinctive mark and since your family knows his birth date," he reasoned aloud, "we can be certain how old he is. We'll send this information to the acoustics lab," Dr. Diaz said. "We'll record his voice on the tape in the acoustic shed, and match it when he comes back each year. You did say he comes back every year, right?"

"He'll be back," Agvik said with certainty. "He always comes back." The boys walked back to their kayak.

Dr. Diaz sat back and pondered what he had just heard.

32

ON THE LAND

———— 2048 ————

By 2048, it had been two hundred years since the first Yankee whale ship sailed into the Arctic. The western Arctic bowhead whale population had recovered its former numbers. The efforts of the Native communities to protect the whales and their habitat had been successful. The sea ice had retreated deep into the high Canadian Arctic in summer. Subarctic whale species like humpback, fin, and even blue whales now frequented the Chukchi and Beaufort seas.

The profitable years of oil development had diminished. Life in the Arctic communities still relied on a subsistence lifestyle . . . without whales, caribou, seals, fish, and the knowledge to hunt them, the village could not survive. Many dog teams were back in use. While still a thriving community, the pace of life had slowed down, and the village people walked the gravel roads of the village, visiting, talking, and sharing food.

Agvik Boyd, now fifty-nine years old, and his crew had become one of the most successful whaling captains in Barrow. He lived on the edge of the village with his family, where he kept a team of twenty dogs. A wind generator powered his house.

"Load that sled with the tent and camping gear, and tie down the *umiaq* to the other sled," called Agvik in a soft but commanding voice.

Emily, now a fit eighty-three-year-old, stood in the yard in her flower-patterned parka as the crew prepared to leave. Following a traditional ceremony, she was handing out candy and snacks to the villagers who had gathered to wish the whaling crews good luck and safety on the ice. She was an esteemed elder in the community and vital as a keeper of traditional knowledge. She knew the land, ice, weather, oral traditions, and traditional skills such as how to make the special waterproof stitches for the sealskin cover on the *umiaq*.

"Be safe, good luck, and may the Lord be with you," she said as the crew departed.

Pulling out of the village, they traveled out onto the shorefast ice to the north and out through the pressure ridges. It was mid-April and the ice was sharp white and blue. Pressure ridges formed mountains of ice that made travel difficult along the narrow trails. The trail was rough but intensely beautiful. The crew and dog team made their way steadily along the bumpy trail with their heavily laden sleds.

They reached the ice edge near the lead edge and set up the camp. The young boys erected the tent and wind-break and chipped out the *aamuaq* or ice ramp where the skin boat would be situated. It was set at the ice edge to launch at a moment's notice. They took the whaling tools from the sled and precisely arranged them in the *umiaq*. Thin headstone-like ice blocks were set along the lead edge to obscure the hunting *umiaq* and camp from the whales' view. After several hours of hard work, they were ready.

Now it was time to wait for the whales. There were over twenty-five thousand bowheads now, but the hunters wanted certain whales—the small whales that provided tender food and were easier to haul onto the ice and butcher. The whole community needed the food these animals provided.

"Look down the lead, about three miles out," said Agvik. His crew turned to see a huge blow.

"Wow, that's a big whale, you can see it forever."

"Too big to harvest," said Agvik.

They watched as the whale approached closer to the camp along the lead edge. The whale had the scars, white peduncle, and completely white flukes showing great age.

Then Agvik became riveted. He knew this whale.

The great whale came close to the crew, right at the lead edge. He spy hopped and exposed its head. There, Agvik saw the white shape of an Eskimo dancer.

Agvik froze, it was Siku. He had not seen him since he was a young man.

He is still alive, he said to himself.

The great whale was now sixty-five feet in length and swam in front of the crew's *umiaq*.

"He is giving himself," Agvik said to himself.

Their eyes met; something deep and primeval passed between them.

The huge exhalations of the whale were almost deafening. He blew in place, not moving; it sprouted seven times in a slow pace with fifteen seconds between blows. Agvik leaned into the skin boat and took out the harpoon and shoulder gun.

The whale sounded briefly and then rose to the surface again in the same position. Water rushed off its back like a surfacing submarine. He was only ten feet from the ice.

Agvik raised the harpoon and then put it down. He nodded at the old whale. Siku blew once more.

"Go, Siku," Agvik spoke quietly. "Watch over us and your whales. We are one."

Later that day, the news went out over the radio that Agvik's crew had caught a small plump whale. It was one of the small bowheads that they called *ingutuks* [ING-gu-tuk] that were the most prized, delicious, and tender. A chorus of cheers and hallelujah chants came from town over the radio. There would be a Nalukataq [NAL-ou-ka-tuk] or "spring whaling" festival that summer where the blanket toss is performed, and the whale is shared. There would be plenty of food for the community. Some would be shared at Nalukataq, and some would be saved for Thanksgiving and Christmas feasts. It would be a good winter in the Arctic.

A NOTE FROM THE EDITOR

Ice Whale is Jean Craighead George's last novel. It was not quite finished when she died last year, so it was completed with the help of two of her children, Twig George, a writer and teacher, and Craig George, a biologist who is an expert on bowhead whales. This book is set in northern Alaska, the same as her classic *Julie of the Wolves.*

Craig George, who lives in Barrow, Alaska, thinks this book about whales was born around the time he was finishing up his PhD dissertation. He says: "I spent three weeks at Mom's place writing in the winter of 2008. She was very taken by my chapter on age estimation and the possibility of two-hundred-year-old bowheads."

Siku, the ice whale of the title, does live for two hundred years, outlasting generations of humans, some who seek to kill him, others to save him—and outlasting the writer who created him as a character. At the time of her death, the book was substantially finished; it had already gone through several revisions. There was no question in the mind of anyone involved, least of all mine, that we would finish the book. Craig George was already fully involved in the project when his mother died; he had been a reader and commentator on the early drafts. I am sure she would have gratefully acknowledged his enormous contributions to this book. I am grateful as well.

We seamed together the plot sections, smoothed the time

line, and corrected some of the geography and science, but it is Jean's voice, lyrical and wondrous when writing about the natural world, that comes through so unmistakably. Simply, Jean George is incomparable.

Lucia Monfried
NOVEMBER *2013*

ACKNOWLEDGMENTS

This book was completed after our mother, Jean George, died in May, 2012. We would like to thank the following people for their help, ideas, and support finishing the text: Lucia Monfried, Cyd Hanns, Gay Sheffield, John Bockstoce, George Noongwook, and T. Luke George. Also many thanks to the amazing Book Club of the Park School: Arenal, Alexa, Isabel, Sarah, Reed, Noam, and Isabelle. Without their wise comments and enthusiasm, this book might never have been completed.

I (Craig) would like to thank the Inupiat and Yup'ik whaling community for teaching me about the sea ice, bowheads, and Arctic life.

We especially thank our mother, Jean, for sharing her love of the natural world and leaving us with this complex "homework assignment," which pulled us together after she died.

Craig George and Twig George
BARROW, ALASKA, AND COCKEYSVILLE, MARYLAND, *2013*

AFTERWORD

~~~~~~~~~~~~

Each spring, over sixteen thousand bowhead whales, or *Aġviq* [Ah-gah-vik] in Inupiat Eskimo, will navigate through fragmentary lanes, called leads, in the sea ice to the Canadian Arctic. There they will feed through the short Arctic summer. The combination of sunlight and nutrients brews a soup of zooplankton on which the bowheads feed. In autumn the herd will begin a feeding migration back to the Bering Sea to winter, as the Arctic Ocean begins to freeze and shut down. The graceful shy bowheads conduct their remarkable annual migratory cycle each year, seeking food and giving birth wary of predators.

The bowhead whale is a large member of the "right whale" family (called Balaenidae), which inhabits the ice-covered seas of the Arctic and sub-Arctic Seas. They can exceed 60 feet (19 m) in body length and 80 tons in body mass, but far larger specimens have been reported by Eskimos and Yankee whalemen in the 1800s.

Remarkably, bowheads begin life in the ice leads along the northwest coast of Alaska. They are the only baleen whale that gives birth in the sub-freezing Arctic waters, and the only one that never leaves the Arctic waters, wintering in the darkness and unimaginable cold of the North Bering Sea. As such, the bowhead has a number of important adaptations: the thickest blubber, greatest longevity, longest baleen, low body core temperatures, and large head-to-body length ratios. All are designed to allow it to live under these extreme conditions. In the words of the Arctic biologist John Burns, "What seems harsh to us, is not harsh for the Arctic animals adapted to live there."

Its baleen is one of its most unusual and important features. Arguably, it is their huge baleen rack that allows the bowhead to thrive in the Arctic seas where food can be very hard to find. Bowheads have about 640 baleen plates in their mouth, divided between two equal-sized racks. Yankee whalers reported baleen to 15 feet in length. The blubber of the bowhead is the thickest of any whale at well over a foot thick in some individuals and comprises up to 50 percent of the body weight.

Another unique thing that sets bowheads apart from other whales is that they are hunted for food by several coastal native communities in Alaska, Russia, and Canada. It is probably true that these Native societies evolved around hunting bowheads and using their products for food, fuel, and building materials. Hunting enormous animals like the bowhead whale requires social coordination, sophisticated tools, and complex hunting strategies. The Inupiat and Yup'ik Eskimos of North America and eastern Asia have hunted bowheads for at least the last two thousand years. Currently in Alaska about forty whales are harvested annually among eleven villages with Barrow taking the most whales.

Yet another unique characteristic of the bowhead, and a major subject of this book, is how long bowheads live. According to the Inupiat, they live "two human lifetimes." According to the scientific research we've conducted with the hunters, lifespans of an astonishing two hundred years are possible.

The knowledge these animals accumulate over two centuries is obviously immense. While no one knows exactly how or what they think, the Inupiat have a strong spiritual connection with the bowhead. It is a mutual exchange. Their belief is a whale only offers itself to a worthy hunter; in exchange the whale earns respect, protection, and an ice cellar with a bed of fresh clean snow as its final resting place. From the western science perspective, their sea ice navigation skills, collective memory of the thousands of places they've successfully found food, and predator avoidance strategies are the kinds of information that bowheads store away. Physiologists also tell us that processing the complex natural sound and communication with other whales may be one of the main functions of their large brains, which are about twice the size of a human brain. While relatively small for an animal that size, their brain retains years of experience and information critical for survival.

Bowheads are able to reproduce to the age of 150 years. A female may give birth to over forty calves in her long life but probably not many survive their early years.

My mother's book captures the severe beauty of the Arctic, follows the bowhead—one of Earth's greatest creatures— and lets us live with the remarkable people who inhabit this land and harvest the whales. She truly loved Barrow and its people. She would visit often and talk in the schools, encouraging young writers. The story is not based on actual events, although it is set in real places and pulls on some of the customs of the indigenous people. At its core, it is her story about the unique and ageless relationship between the Eskimo people and the bowhead whale. It is also about the Arctic's uncertain future.

While some find it ironic, it should be no surprise that no one has fought harder to protect the bowhead and its habitat than the Inupiat and Yup'ik Eskimo whalers. We should all applaud their dedication and hope that their relationship with the bowhead will persist another two thousand years. While they've continued to hunt, bowheads have nearly recovered to their former population size and now number seventeen thousand strong in the western Arctic alone. Now science shows us that the main threat to the survival of whales is no longer commercial whaling; instead it is the cumulative sum of shipping, pollution, climate change, commercial fishing, offshore oil development, other human activities, and even, to a small degree, whale watching. As the Inupiat say, *aġvikseoksagatagichi* (Keep on whaling)."

John Craighead "Craig" George Ph.D.
BARROW, ALASKA
2013

TURN THE PAGE FOR AN EXCERPT
FROM JEAN CRAIGHEAD GEORGE'S ICONIC STORY
ABOUT COURAGE, DANGER, AND INDEPENDENCE:

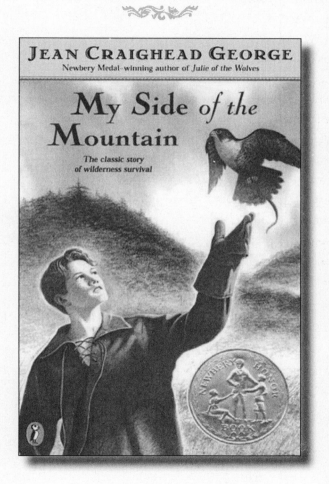

I Hole Up in a Snowstorm

I am on my mountain in a tree home that people have passed without ever knowing that I am here. The house is a hemlock tree six feet in diameter, and must be as old as the mountain itself. I came upon it last summer and dug and burned it out until I made a snug cave in the tree that I now call home.

"My bed is on the right as you enter, and is made of ash slats and covered with deerskin. On the left is a small fireplace about knee high. It is of clay and stones. It has a chimney that leads the smoke out through a knothole. I chipped out three other knotholes to let fresh air in. The air coming in is bitter cold. It must be below zero outside, and yet I can sit here inside my tree and write with bare hands. The fire is small, too. It doesn't take much fire to warm this tree room.

"It is the fourth of December, I think. It may be the fifth. I am not sure because I have not recently counted the notches in the aspen pole that is my calendar. I have been just too busy gathering nuts and berries, smoking venison, fish, and small game to keep up with the exact date.

"The lamp I am writing by is deer fat poured into a turtle shell with a strip of my old city trousers for a wick.

"It snowed all day yesterday and today. I have not been outside since the storm began, and I am bored for the first time since I ran away from home eight months ago to live on the land.

"I am well and healthy. The food is good. Sometimes I eat turtle soup, and I know how to make acorn pancakes. I keep my supplies in the wall of the tree in wooden pockets that I chopped myself.

"Every time I have looked at those pockets during the last two days, I have felt just like a squirrel, which reminds me: I didn't see a squirrel one whole day before that storm began. I guess they are holed up and eating their stored nuts, too.

"I wonder if The Baron, that's the wild weasel who lives behind the big boulder to the north of my tree, is also denned up. Well, anyway, I think the storm is dying down because the tree is not crying so much. When the wind really blows, the whole tree moans right down to the roots, which is where I am.

"Tomorrow I hope The Baron and I can tunnel out into the sunlight. I wonder if I should dig the snow. But that would mean I would have to put it somewhere, and the only place to put it is in my nice snug tree.

Maybe I can pack it with my hands as I go. I've always dug into the snow from the top, never up from under.

"The Baron must dig up from under the snow. I wonder where he puts what he digs? Well, I guess I'll know in the morning."

When I wrote that last winter, I was scared and thought maybe I'd never get out of my tree. I had been scared for two days—ever since the first blizzard hit the Catskill Mountains. When I came up to the sunlight, which I did by simply poking my head into the soft snow and standing up, I laughed at my dark fears.

Everything was white, clean, shining, and beautiful. The sky was blue, blue, blue. The hemlock grove was laced with snow, the meadow was smooth and white, and the gorge was sparkling with ice. It was so beautiful and peaceful that I laughed out loud. I guess I laughed because my first snowstorm was over and it had not been so terrible after all.

Then I shouted, "I did it!" My voice never got very far. It was hushed by the tons of snow.

I looked for signs from The Baron Weasel. His footsteps were all over the boulder, also slides where he had played. He must have been up for hours, enjoying the new snow.

Inspired by his fun, I poked my head into my tree and whistled. Frightful, my trained falcon, flew to my fist, and we jumped and slid down the mountain, making big

holes and trenches as we went. It was good to be whistling and carefree again, because I was sure scared by the coming of that storm.

I had been working since May, learning how to make a fire with flint and steel, finding what plants I could eat, how to trap animals and catch fish—all this so that when the curtain of blizzard struck the Catskills, I could crawl inside my tree and be comfortably warm and have plenty to eat.

During the summer and fall I had thought about the coming of winter. However, on that third day of December when the sky blackened, the temperature dropped, and the first flakes swirled around me. I must admit that I wanted to run back to New York. Even the first night that I spent out in the woods, when I couldn't get the fire started, was not as frightening as the snowstorm that gathered behind the gorge and mushroomed up over my mountain.

I was smoking three trout. It was nine o'clock in the morning. I was busy keeping the flames low so they would not leap up and burn the fish. As I worked, it occurred to me that it was awfully dark for that hour of the morning. Frightful was leashed to her tree stub. She seemed restless and pulled at her tethers. Then I realized that the forest was dead quiet. Even the woodpeckers that had been tapping around me all morning were silent. The squirrels were nowhere to be seen. The juncos and chickadees and nuthatches were gone. I looked to see what The Baron Weasel was doing. He was not around. I looked up.

From my tree you can see the gorge beyond the meadow. White water pours between the black wet

boulders and cascades into the valley below. The water
that day was as dark as the rocks. Only the sound told
me it was still falling. Above the darkness stood another
darkness. The clouds of winter, black and fearsome.
They looked as wild as the winds that were bringing
them. I grew sick with fright. I knew I had enough food.
I knew everything was going to be perfectly all right.
But knowing that didn't help. I was scared. I stamped
out the fire and pocketed the fish.

I tried to whistle for Frightful, but couldn't purse my
shaking lips tight enough to get out anything but *pfffff.*
So I grabbed her by the hide straps that are attached to
her legs and we dove through the deerskin door into my
room in the tree.

I put Frightful on the bedpost, and curled up in a ball
on the bed. I thought about New York and the noise
and the lights and how a snowstorm always seemed very
friendly there. I thought about our apartment, too. At
that moment it seemed bright and lighted and warm. I
had to keep saying to myself: There were eleven of us
in it! Dad, Mother, four sisters, four brothers, and me.
And not one of us liked it, except perhaps little Nina,
who was too young to know. Dad didn't like it even a
little bit. He had been a sailor once, but when I was
born, he gave up the sea and worked on the docks in
New York. Dad didn't like the land. He liked the sea,
wet and big and endless.

Sometimes he would tell me about Great-grandfather
Gribley, who owned land in the Catskill Mountains and

felled the trees and built a home and plowed the land—only to discover that he wanted to be a sailor. The farm failed, and Great-grandfather Gribley went to sea.

As I lay with my face buried in the sweet greasy smell of my deerskin, I could hear Dad's voice saying, "That land is still in the family's name. Somewhere in the Catskills is an old beech with the name *Gribley* carved on it. It marks the northern boundary of Gribley's folly—the land is no place for a Gribley."

"The land is no place for a Gribley," I said. "The land is no place for a Gribley, and here I am three hundred feet from the beech with *Gribley* carved on it."

I fell asleep at that point, and when I awoke I was hungry. I cracked some walnuts, got down the acorn flour I had pounded, with a bit of ash to remove the bite, reached out the door for a little snow, and stirred up some acorn pancakes. I cooked them on a top of a tin can, and as I ate them, smothered with blueberry jam, I knew that the land was just the place for a Gribley.

IN WHICH
I Get Started on This Venture

I left New York in May. I had a penknife, a ball of cord, an ax, and $40, which I had saved from selling magazine subscriptions. I also had some flint and steel which

I had bought at a Chinese store in the city. The man in the store had showed me how to use it. He had also given me a little purse to put it in, and some tinder to catch the sparks. He had told me that if I ran out of tinder, I should burn cloth, and use the charred ashes.

I thanked him and said, "This is the kind of thing I am not going to forget."

On the train north to the Catskills I unwrapped my flint and steel and practiced hitting them together to make sparks. On the wrapping paper I made these notes.

"A hard brisk strike is best. Remember to hold the steel in the left hand and the flint in the right, and hit the steel with the flint.

"The trouble is the sparks go every which way."

And that *was* the trouble. I did not get a fire going that night, and as I mentioned, this was a scary experience.

I hitched rides into the Catskill Mountains. At about four o'clock a truck driver and I passed through a beautiful dark hemlock forest, and I said to him, "This is as far as I am going."

He looked all around and said, "You live here?"

"No," I said, "but I am running away from home, and this is just the kind of forest I have always dreamed I would run to. I think I'll camp here tonight." I hopped out of the cab.

"Hey, boy," the driver shouted. "Are you serious?"

"Sure," I said.

"Well, now, ain't that sumpin'? You know, when I was your age, I did the same thing. Only thing was, I was a farm boy and ran to the city, and you're a city boy running to the woods. I was scared of the city—do you think you'll be scared of the woods?"

"Heck, no!" I shouted loudly.

As I marched into the cool shadowy woods, I heard the driver call to me, "I'll be back in the morning, if you want to ride home."

He laughed. Everybody laughed at me. Even Dad. I told Dad that I was going to run away to Great-grand-father Gribley's land. He had roared with laughter and told me about the time he had run away from home. He got on a boat headed for Singapore, but when the whistle blew for departure, he was down the gangplank and home in bed before anyone knew he was gone. Then he told me, "Sure, go try it. Every boy should try it."

I must have walked a mile into the woods until I found a stream. It was a clear athletic stream that rushed and ran and jumped and splashed. Ferns grew along its bank, and its rocks were upholstered with moss.

I sat down, smelled the piney air, and took out my penknife. I cut off a green twig and began to whittle. I have always been good at whittling. I carved a ship once that my teacher exhibited for parents' night at school.

whittle angles — sharpen — string →

wooden fishhook

First I whittled an angle on one end of the twig. Then I cut a smaller twig and sharpened it to a point. I whittled an angle on that twig, and bound the two angles face to face with a strip of green bark. It was supposed to be a fishhook.

According to a book on how to survive on the land that I read in the New York Public Library, this was the way to make your own hooks. I then dug for worms. I had hardly chopped the moss away with my ax before I hit frost. It had not occurred to me that there would be frost in the ground in May, but then, I had not been on a mountain before.

This did worry me, because I was depending on fish to keep me alive until I got to my great-grandfather's mountain, where I was going to make traps and catch game.

I looked into the stream to see what else I could eat, and as I did, my hand knocked a rotten log apart. I remembered about old logs and all the sleeping stages of insects that are in it. I chopped away until I found a cold white grub.

I swiftly tied a string to my hook, put the grub on, and walked up the stream looking for a good place to fish. All the manuals I had read were very emphatic about where fish lived, and so I had memorized this: "In streams, fish usually congregate in pools and deep calm water. The heads of riffles, small rapids, the tail of a pool, eddies below rocks or logs, deep undercut banks, in the shade of overhanging bushes—all are very likely places to fish."

This stream did not seem to have any calm water, and I must have walked a thousand miles before I found a pool by a deep undercut bank in the shade of overhanging bushes. Actually, it wasn't that far, it just seemed that way because as I went looking and finding nothing, I was sure I was going to starve to death.

I squatted on this bank and dropped in my line. I did so want to catch a fish. One fish would set me upon my way, because I had read how much you can learn from one fish. By examining the contents of its stomach you can find what the other fish are eating or you can use the internal organs as bait.

The grub went down to the bottom of the stream. It swirled around and hung still. Suddenly the string came

to life, and rode back and forth and around in a circle. I pulled with a powerful jerk. The hook came apart, and whatever I had went circling back to its bed.

Well, that almost made me cry. My bait was gone, my hook was broken, and I was getting cold, frightened, and mad. I whittled another hook, but this time I cheated and used string to wind it together instead of bark. I walked back to the log and luckily found another grub. I hurried to the pool, and I flipped a trout out of the water before I knew I had a bite.

The fish flopped, and I threw my whole body over it. I could not bear to think of it flopping itself back into the stream.

I cleaned it like I had seen the man at the fish market do, examined its stomach, and found it empty. This horrified me. What I didn't know was that an empty stomach means the fish are hungry and will eat about anything. However, I thought at the time that I was a goner. Sadly, I put some of the internal organs on my hook, and before I could get my line to the bottom I had another bite. I lost that one, but got the next one. I stopped when I had five nice little trout and looked around for a place to build a camp and make a fire.

It wasn't hard to find a pretty spot along that stream. I selected a place beside a mossy rock in a circle of hemlocks.

I decided to make a bed before I cooked. I cut off some boughs for a mattress, then I leaned some dead limbs against the boulder and covered them with hemlock limbs. This made a kind of tent. I crawled in, lay down, and felt alone and secret and very excited.

But ah, the rest of this story! I was on the northeast side of the mountain. It grew dark and cold early. Seeing the shadows slide down on me, I frantically ran around gathering firewood. This is about the only thing

a couple of good shelters - make sure your fire is on scraped earth - also be sure to put it out!

I did right from that moment until dawn, because I remembered that the driest wood in a forest is the dead limbs that are still on the trees, and I gathered an enormous pile of them. That pile must still be there, for I never got a fire going.